Undertaker's Match

Stephanie Webb Dillon

Copyright © 2023 by Stephanie Webb Dillon

All rights reserved.

No part of this publication may be reproduced, distributed, or transmitted in any form or by any means, including photocopying, recording, or other electronic or mechanical methods, without the prior written permission of the publisher, except as permitted by U.S. copyright law. For permission requests, contact [include publisher/author contact info].

The story, all names, characters, and incidents portrayed in this production are fictitious. No identification with actual persons (living or deceased), places, buildings, and products is intended or should be inferred.

Book Cover by RLS Images, Graphics & Design/ Michelle RLS Sewell

Photographer: Eric Mulroney

Cover Model: Jose L. Barreiro

First edition 2023

Also By

Freedom Colorado Series:
Baked with Love
Playing for Keeps
Sheriff's Convenient Bride
Daddy's Second Chance
The Scars Within
Guarding her Heart

Men of Phoenix Security:
Hidden Desires
Uncovering her Secrets

Rippers' MC:
Undertaker's Match

SAMHSA'S (Substance Abuse and Mental Health Services Administration) National Helpline, 1-800-662-HELP (4357). (also known as the Treatment Referral Routing Service), or TTY: 1-800-487-4889 is a confidential, free 24-hour-a-day, 365-day a-year information service, in English and Spanish, for individuals and family members facing mental and/or substance use disorders. This service provides referrals to local treatment facilities, support groups, and community-based organizations.

Also visit the online treatment locator or send your zip code via text message: 435748 (HELP4U) to find help near you.

I have included this information as a way to hopefully reach out to those in need. My daughter is an addict, I pray for her every day that she will get help. She has lost many friends to suicide and overdose. If this helps anyone then it is worth it.

1

Zeke

It was a Friday night the week before Thanksgiving and things had been good for our MC lately. The guys were having a party tonight. The kind of party that I haven't participated in since before Lisa. There will be club whores there ready to service anyone that wants them and orgies going on in the common area. There were no old ladies around anymore since most of the older members had passed or were not able to be active anymore. I guess I was the oldest member, hell I was only forty-eight, not that damn old but older than the twenty-five to forty year old guys in the club now. Fang and Brody were the closest to my age and then Axle. Axle had been like a brother to my VP's son, Bear. They grew up together at the clubhouse along with Bear's sister Valkyrie. What happened to her was a fucking tragedy. Women were meant to be treasured and protected. I'm just glad we were able to finish off the bastards that hurt her. A few years ago, my old lady, Lisa, had been diagnosed with bone cancer. It was horrible to watch her suffer. I ended up turning the MC over to Axle who had been my VP for a several years. I had to be home to take care of my wife. She needed me and I needed to spend as much time with her as she had left. That was the longest and shortest six months of my life. When she died, I wanted to crawl into a bottle and go with her. I got stupid drunk one night and almost shot myself. I sat in the dark crying and holding the damn gun to my head, hands shaking when I realized what a pussy I was being. Lisa would have kicked my ass if she could have seen me wasting my life when hers was stolen by that horrible disease. That was my wake-up call, I took a shower and drank a pot of coffee trying to sober up and then slept. When I woke up, I went into town and found an AA meeting. I called Axle and asked him to go through my house and pour out all the liquor. I told him all of my hiding spots. I was afraid that if I came home and it was there, I would be tempted to drink.

The first month I went to a meeting every day. I was slowly getting better and able to space them out more. My friends' son Bear was married, and his woman was about to have triplets. I wanted to be there for them. Be an uncle. I was never able to be a father, Lisa couldn't have children and I loved her enough to accept it. She mothered the hell out of the young prospects and Bear, Axle and Valkyrie any time they were at the club. She always fed them and made sure they had whatever they needed. I loved that woman like no other and I can't imagine loving anyone else that way. Several months ago, I got to know Stone's girl, Lucy and her daughter Sarah. That little one wrapped me around her finger so fast. I started to think that maybe I could have some happiness again. I knew that Lisa didn't want me to be alone the rest of my life. I think James was trying to fix me up with his mother. While she was a lovely woman, she really wasn't my type. She was very independent and self-sufficient. I wanted a woman who needed me. Someone who wanted to be coddled, cared for, protected and loved beyond measure. I wanted someone I could spoil. I knew a few of the guys in the club were 'Daddies', but that level of age play didn't interest me. I was dominant in the bedroom, and I wanted a submissive who would be mine to take care of. I just haven't found her yet. I was watching a fight on tv eating some leftover pizza when I heard a knock at my door. With a sigh I got up to see who it was.

2

Zeke

I opened the door and standing on my porch was a woman who looked vaguely familiar, but I couldn't place her. Thinking she was probably one of the club whores that hung around I didn't want her getting any ideas.

"How did you get on the property?" I asked her. She looked at me and frowned then stepped past me into my house. "I didn't invite you in Miss?"

She turned on me at that moment and I saw her pregnant belly. I looked at her and my cock got hard instantly. She was petite maybe five foot two inches tall with long, wavy strawberry-blonde hair and her eyes were the brightest blue I had ever seen. I was dumbstruck. Then I registered that she was pregnant.

"You don't fucking remember me, do you?" she said sounding hurt and then pissed. "Damnit, I knew you had been drinking that night, but you didn't seem blackout drunk. Well hell, there is no easy way to say this but I'm pregnant with your child. I'm six months pregnant and I thought you should know."

"Bullshit." I said to her, thinking no way in hell I didn't use a condom with her if I did fuck her. "I never fuck ungloved."

"Well, you are the only man I have ever been with, so you win the daddy lottery." she said sharply. She looked me up and down and then straight in my eyes. "At least you're sober now."

"Little girl, I don't know who you think you're pulling one over on, but it won't be me. I'll give you five minutes to get back in your car and go back to where you came from." I said as I escorted her out and closed the door. Seriously, why did women think we were such easy targets. The damn hard cock in my pants is why. I ran my hand through my hair and started to sit back down when I realized that I didn't hear a car. What I heard was someone stomping away and then a scream. Well fuck. I threw on my boots and went outside to see one of the prospects had his hands on her and she was trying to fight him off. That pissed me off and threw all my protective instincts into high gear.

"Get your hands off of her boy or you're going to be in deep shit." I told him as I grabbed his shirt and pulled him off of her. I hated to see a woman manhandled like that and I could tell he had scared her.

"Mind your business old man, the whore wants it, or she wouldn't be here." The little punk started to grab her again and I laid him out. Pulling my phone out of my pocket I called Gator who was on gate duty.

"Gator, get your ass to my house and get this piece of shit prospect off our property. I don't know the little shit's name, but he was getting handsy with someone who didn't want it and he was disrespecting me. Once you see who he is I want Axle made aware and I never want to see him here again." I looked over and saw her shirt was torn and she was shaking and crying. I looked around and didn't see a car anywhere. "Miss how did you get here?"

"My name is Annie, and I don't have a car. I lost my job because I keep getting sick and I got kicked out of my rental because I don't have money to pay my rent. I know I was nothing special that night. I was just tired of being alone and you were handsome and charming. When I found out I was pregnant I was going to handle it alone, but I can't now. I need help." She whispered as she sat on the ground, wrapped her arms around herself and rocked.

"Don't you have parents or some family that you can stay with?" I asked her, feeling like an ass. I still didn't really believe the baby was mine. It was obvious the girl was knocked up though.

"I don't have anybody." She told me in a defeated voice then took a deep breath, got up and started walking toward the gate, she made it about ten feet when she collapsed. My heart stopped as I ran over to her and picked her up. Jesus, she didn't weigh anything even for a pregnant girl. I carried her inside my house and laid her in the guest room. I turned on the bedside lamp and looked her over. She was breathing but she was pale and had dark circles under her eyes. She looked very thin and malnourished. This wouldn't do at all. Picking up my phone I sent a text to Doc, hopefully he wasn't balls deep in a whore right now. I saw a response saying he would be here in ten minutes. I told him to come on in when he got here. I didn't feel right leaving her alone. I heard the screen door open and close.

"What the hell is this Undertaker?" Doc asked as ran his hand through his hair and came over to check on her.

"She collapsed outside, she is claiming the baby is mine. Right now, I just need to know what's wrong with her." I told him, stepping back to give him room. He picked up her wrist and checked her pulse and then used smelling salts to wake her up. She startled awake and looked at Doc with panic on her face. "Easy Annie, it's okay. This here is Doc, he is just checking on you."

She looked up at him and glanced back at me. I walked around to the other side of the bed and sat down offering her my hand.

"Annie, I just need to ask you a few questions. I would really like to take you to my clinic for an ultrasound and some tests. Undertaker here, tells me you are pregnant. I can tell by looking at you that you are not getting enough sleep and you are malnourished. That is not good for the baby." Doc said frowning at me.

"Don't look at me like that I just found out." I said defensively. "I'll meet you at your clinic, let's go." I started to help her up, but she just whimpered.

"I don't have any money or health insurance. I can't afford tests and stuff." she said with tears dripping down her face again. When she looked back up at me with her bright blue eyes swimming in tears, I knew I was done for, there was no way I could turn her away. I sighed and looked at Doc.

"Honey, don't worry. I'm not planning to charge you. I do a lot of pro bono work. I have free clinic days. Let's go get you and the little one checked out. You want a healthy baby, right?" he prompted her gently. She nodded and slowly got off the bed. I saw she was about to go down and scooped her up into my arms.

"Doc, will you grab my keys off the counter." I asked as I walked towards the door with her. She laid her head against my shoulder. That worried me because she'd had more fight in her when she got here. Now she just seemed small, exhausted and resigned. I put her in my truck and buckled her in, took my keys from Doc and drove to the clinic just outside of the property. Glancing over at her every few minutes to make sure she had not slumped over again. Even as sick as she was I still thought she was one of the most beautiful women I had ever seen.

3

*A*nnie

I was fading in and out on the ride to the clinic. I was so tired, and I had no energy. I had tried to take care of myself but between not being able to keep food down and then losing my job I had no money. I stayed at the shelter for a few days, but they didn't have an available bed tonight. I was out of options, so I came looking for my baby daddy. I knew he was part of the MC outside of town. Many of them frequented the bar where I had been working. Jakes was definitely a biker bar, but I used to make really good tips when I could work my full shifts. Losing that job was hard because I wasn't qualified to do anything else. My mother died when I was six and my father had remarried a few years ago. His wife didn't like having me around, so she made my life miserable. He pulled up outside the clinic and came around to get me out. I wanted to argue that I could walk but who was I kidding. I had already collapsed twice so I let him pick me up and carry me inside. I wouldn't tell him, but it felt so good to be in his arms. He may not remember that night, but I will never forget it. It was the best night of my life. I was mortified and humiliated when he left the next morning while I was asleep and didn't leave a note or anything. I had not seen him since.

"Put her on the table, I'll get a gown for her. You will have to help her change since she doesn't have the strength to do it herself." Doc said to Zeke as he handed me a gown and a sheet. "I'll be back in a few minutes with the ultrasound machine."

I looked at the gown for a few minutes and started trying to take my clothes off. I was so weak I was struggling. I heard him curse under his breath and then he started to help me. I wasn't wearing a bra but then I didn't need one. He slid the gown around me loosely tying it in the front.

"Lay down so he can check you over." Zeke grumbled. I lay back on the exam table and looked at him as he paced. At first glance all you see is a rough biker who seems hard and cold. I knew he was older, but he was still striking and in amazing shape. You would never know by glancing at him that the man had abs of steel. He had been so sweet to me that night and I could tell he was lonely. Since I was too, I took him back to my place. We went at it for hours before I passed out exhausted from all the orgasms, he gave me. The Doc came back in, and I blushed at my thoughts.

"Ok, let's see what we have here." Doc raised my gown off of my stomach and put some warm gel over it, then started to move the wand around. Suddenly we heard a fast woosh woosh and Doc pointed at the heart beating. "Looks like the little peanut is doing fine, do you want to know the sex?"

Zeke's eyes got really big, and I nodded my head as he squeezed my hand. We both looked at the screen. He waved it over an area, and I realized what I was looking at.

"It's a boy. I'm going to print out a couple of these for you, then we need to draw some blood to test everything else. I'm also going to do an amniocentesis to check for any abnormalities as well as do a paternity test." Doc pulled out all the instruments he needed and a couple of blood drawing kits. He gently took my arm and found a vein. After getting my blood, he took a sample of Zeke's. Then he cleaned off my stomach with alcohol.

"This one you have to be very still for. I'll have Undertaker here hold your hand and if you get nervous squeeze it. You will feel a little pinch." He told me gently as he looked at me. Zeke moved to where I was and sat closer to my head and held my hand while stroking my hair. Doc was very quick about it then cleaned the spot. "Ok, we are all done now. I should have the results in a few days since I am putting a rush on them. Where will you be staying Annie?"

I felt sick because I didn't have anywhere to stay and while Zeke was being nice now, he had made it abundantly clear what he thought of my predicament. I felt tears well in my eyes and I turned my head trying to blink them back. I just shook my head.

"She will be at my place." Zeke told Doc as he got my clothes to help me back into them. Doc stepped out so that he could help me dress. Helping me to my feet, he kept his arm around me as we walked into his office.

"I have a prescription for some prenatal vitamins, and I have a sample here for you to go ahead and take along with something to help with the nausea. Have her eat smaller meals throughout the day and get some ginger ale and crackers in her before she tries to get out of bed. We need to get her weight up. I'll call you in a couple of days with the results." Doc said as he handed Zeke a small bag and walked us to the door.

4

Zeke

She was very quiet on the drive back to my place. I glanced over at her a couple of times and she just stared blankly out the window. I hated to admit it, but I believe her. She didn't protest the paternity test once. I'm going to be a father. Forty-eight fucking years old and now I'm going to have a kid. Geez, and with a woman almost half my age. What the hell was I thinking sleeping with her in the first place. I just wish I could remember it. It must have been the night before I decided to get sober. I knew I was messed up and not thinking clearly. She is so different from my Lisa; she had been full of piss and vinegar but would mother all the guys to death. She never took any of my shit. Annie, on the other hand, seemed to shy away from confrontation and she didn't seem to have anyone to care for her.

I pulled up the house and shut off the engine. She had fallen asleep again. I leaned over and gently settled her against the back of the seat so I could get the door open. Walking around I picked her up and snagged the bag of vitamins carrying her inside. I took her to the guest room and laid her down. Covering her up with a blanket, I then slipped off her socks and shoes. I left the bedside lamp on low and cracked the door. Exhausted, I pulled off my own socks, shoes and T-shirt and crawled into my own bed to sleep.

I jumped up when I heard a scream from the next room. I ran into her room, and she was sitting up looking out at nothing. Clearly, she was having a night terror, sighing I walked over and sat down beside her.

"Annie, honey go back to sleep. You're safe here." I whispered as I rubbed her back gently. She blinked a few times and glanced up at me. Suddenly she was wrapped around me like a monkey.

"You're really here, I'm not alone. I thought I was dreaming and then suddenly I was on the street with our baby, we were both starving and cold." She was trembling and whimpering against me. I scooted back against the headboard and gently eased her into a reclining position against me.

"I'm here, you're not going anywhere. I'm going to take care of you both, now go back to sleep and we will take this one day at a time." I said softly as I stroked her hair. Her whimpers quieted as she fell asleep in my arms. I reached for the blanket and pulled it over us. Holding her felt so good. I haven't slept with a woman in my arms in over a year. Before I knew it, I had dozed off too.

I woke up to the feel of Annie nuzzling my chest, glancing down I saw her eyes still closed. I stared at the way her lashes looked against her creamy skin, her rosy lips in a cupid's bow and the little dimple in her chin. Her tiny hand was curled under her chin as she snuggled closer. I touched her hair gently; it looked like it needed a good wash and brushing out. I knew I wasn't going back to sleep. I eased out from under her, putting a pillow in my place. I went to take a shower and get dressed.

Standing in front of the mirror, I decided to trim up my beard. I was getting dressed when I heard her feet shuffling in the hall. I stepped out with the towel around my neck and my jeans on to see her run past me and kneel in front of the toilet to get sick. I reached behind the door and got a washcloth to wet it in the sink. I knelt beside her and pulled her hair back for her wiping her head and handing her the cloth when she sat back on her heels.

"I want you to stay right here, sit on this towel and I will be back in a minute with some crackers. I need to go pick up some ginger ale." He handed her a folded towel to sit on and then headed to the kitchen. Mercy, throwing on a T-shirt he grabbed his phone and called Axle.

"Hey Taker, what's up?" he asked when he answered the phone. "I heard you have some company at your place."

"Not talking about that right now. I need you to run to the store for me and pick up a couple of boxes of saltine crackers and a couple of twelve packs of ginger ale." I told him as I walked back to the bathroom with a sleeve of crackers and a cup of ice water. "See you shortly."

"Yes sir. See you soon." Axle said as he hung up. Slipping my phone in my pocket I opened the crackers, handing her a few.

"Honey, eat a couple of these slowly and then take small sips of the water. Let me know when you think you can move." I leaned against the bathroom counter. She nibbled on the crackers and drank some of the water. Looking up at him she squirmed a little and looked at the toilet. "You need to use the toilet huh."

She nodded looking embarrassed. I got up and stepped out for a minute. When I heard the flush, I went back in.

"I have a pair of sweats, a t-shirt and a hoodie you can put on if you would like to take a shower." I suggested laying the clothes on the counter. She looked longingly at the shower and then gave me a small smile.

"Yes please. I just don't know if I have the energy to do it." She was blushing and looking down at her belly.

"Annie, we both know I have seen it all before. Would you like me to help you take a bath and wash your hair for you?" I offered. I wondered if she would throw something at me, but she just nodded and stepped into me to hug me. "Okay honey, sit down here while I start the water. Why don't you go ahead and take those clothes off?"

She stood up and dropped her pants and then sat back down as she peeled the shirt over her head. She had bruised on her arms like handprints. I swore and she looked up at me with her eyes wide. Once I got the water to the right temperature, I put some bubble bath in that I found under the cabinet. Then I gently picked her up and settled her in the tub.

"I'm so sorry he did that to you. If I had just listened to you that would not have happened. I wish I had hit him harder." I frowned, grabbing the body wash and squirting some on a washcloth. This girl was getting to me, and I didn't like it a bit. I started to gently wash her back, then her neck, and shoulders. As I started down to her front I paused, and her breath hitched. She looked up at me and nodded. I continued to wash her trying to be clinical about it and pretend that my dick wasn't hard as a rock wanting out of my pants. Try to pretend that I didn't want to lean over and take those breasts with my mouth and tongue. I took a deep breath and washed her legs. I started to hand her the washcloth so she could wash her pussy and she didn't take it. She took my hand and put it on her using me to wash herself. I was shaking with the urge to take her. I glanced up at her and her eyes were glazed with lust. She leaned over and pressed her lips to mine. I kissed her and pulled back.

"That's not what this is about, honey. Let's get your hair washed." I told her as I picked up the cup I brought in and filled it with water from the spout. "Scoot up a little and tilt your head back." She did what I said, and I poured the water over her hair making sure it was all saturated. Then I took the shampoo and worked it into her hair massaging her scalp as I did it and working it to the ends, I rinsed it and did it again. After working some conditioner through her hair, I helped her rinse it all out then helped her out of the tub. I handed her my robe to put on and found a wide tooth comb in the drawer that I could use on her hair.

"Sit on the ottoman in front of the big chair. I'm going to comb your hair out for you." I led her over to it and I sat in the chair behind her. I used to do Lisa's hair all the time, so I knew to be gentle and not pull. Definitely didn't have to worry about getting them mixed up in my head. My Lisa had blonde hair, where Annie's is like a sunset. I sprayed some detangler that I found in the cabinet, it was old but I'm sure it would still help. After separating it into sections I got to work.

5

Annie

I sat Indian style on the ottoman with this man's robe wrapped around my body. I could smell him on it, and I was trying hard not to bury my nose in it and take deep breaths. He was such a contradiction. He looked mean, hard and could be very gruff. Then he did stuff like this. Taking care of me, bathing me and he was combing my hair. I expected him to jerk and pull but no, he held my hair in his hands towards the ends and gently worked the comb through being careful not to hurt me. I had not had anyone take care of me in years. My grandmother raised me after my mother took off, no idea who my father was. When Nana passed a few years ago, I was on my own, she had left me a little cash but having been in financial trouble she had a reverse mortgage, so the bank took our home.

I didn't release how deep in thought I was because suddenly he was finished, and my hair was in a long French braid down my back. I reached back to touch it and turned to look at the man who did it. He was watching me carefully.

"Do you think you could eat some scrambled eggs and toast if I fixed them?" he asked me as he got up from the chair.

"I'll try, I'm going to go put some clothes on." I told him as I walked to the bedroom and found my backpack. I didn't have much, I pulled out some leggings, clean underwear and a threadbare long sleeve waffle shirt I had. I really needed clothes. These leggings were so stretched out from my pregnancy they barely stayed up. I looked over at the clothes he had given me to wear and decided they would be much warmer. I hung his robe up in the bathroom and came back to the living room. Zeke was at the stove finishing the eggs and plating them along with some toast. My stomach growled. I blushed and went to sit at the table. When he placed the plate in front of me, he sat a glass of milk down too.

"Try to eat and drink as much as you can but slowly. We need to get you and little man healthy." He grumbled as he sat beside me to eat. I watched him as I ate and thought about what a sexy man he was. I never thought I would be attracted to a man that much older than me, but he was a beautiful man. I can imagine what he might have looked like younger without the white beard and the silver streaking his dark hair. His eyes were dark but expressive, his body was covered in tattoos and the muscles were just delicious to behold. I seemed to be Perma horny with this pregnancy. The eggs were good, and the toast was just what I needed. I finished all of it and slowly sipped on my milk.

"Thank you for breakfast and well everything." I whispered suddenly feeling very self-conscious about having to depend on him for so much. "I'll pay you back for everything as soon as I can find a job."

"Your only job for the next four months is growing our son and taking care of yourself and then after you will take time to heal. I have plenty of room and you need looking after." He said firmly as he took our plates to rinse them out. I started to say something when someone knocked at the door. Zeke hollered for him to come in.

"Hey Taker, I've got the groceries you asked for." The handsome guy with the van dyke beard and dark hair glanced over at me in surprise. "Well, hello lovely, how are you this morning?" he said to me as he winked. Zeke growled and the guy laughed.

"Hi, I know I've seen you before, but I don't remember your name." I told him quietly. "You came into Jakes' with some of your friends."

"Oh yeah, you must be Annie. They all said you were the best waitress there." He said as he helped put away the groceries. "This guy taking good care of you?"

"He is, thanks." I told him before getting up to go to the bathroom. I barely sat on the toilet when there was a light knock on the door.

"Are you okay?" Zeke asked through the door. I smiled to myself; it was sweet he was worried that I was losing my breakfast.

"I'm good just need to pee, baby is dancing on my bladder. Be right out." I told him as I waited for him to move away before I flushed the toilet and washed my hands. I looked in the mirror and cringed. My face was pale, and I had circles under my eyes. I walked out and right into a hard chest. His arms flew around me to steady me. I glanced up at him and he was looking at my lips. I wanted him so badly, but he didn't even remember being with me. I was that unmemorable. I suddenly felt cold and stepped back walking out of the room. My heart was too vulnerable to allow myself to entertain thoughts of being with this man again. I turned and went into the guest room, closed the door and laid down.

I heard the men talking but didn't really know what they were saying. I really didn't care, I just wanted to sleep. I was still so tired, and I wasn't sure how long this reprieve would last. I mean he seems to believe the baby is his, but what does that even mean. I don't want to be a charity case. I just need to find work and a place I can afford to live until I have the baby. Maybe I could find a roommate. Closing my eyes, I curled up against the pillow he had laid on the night before and fell into a fitful sleep.

6

Zeke

I'm not sure what happened. One minute she was in my arms and the next she was running away like a scalded cat. I started to follow her but saw her go into the guest room and close the door. Clearly, she did not want me to follow her. I ran my hand through my hair and went back to the living room. Axle was standing in the kitchen sipping a cup of coffee. He looked at me, smirked and shook his head.

"So, what are you going to do with her?" he asked me, sitting down at the table. "She is obviously pregnant. I'm guessing it's yours since she is here. I remember seeing her at Jakes' plenty of times. I've never seen her hook up with anyone."

"Yeah, apparently it happened the night before I decided to get help and sober up. My headfuck is that I don't have any memory of it, but she took the paternity test without even blinking. She is confident that the baby is mine. She is also jobless and homeless due to being so sick with her pregnancy so I can't very well put her out."

"Yeah, and I remember that night very well, you were shitfaced when you went to Jakes'. I remember you leaving about closing but you didn't come home until the next morning." Axle got up and rinsed his coffee cup out. "I was going to start looking for someone to work at the front desk at the garage. Kelly quit a few days ago, something about going back home to Montana. It's easy work, she can sit down her whole shift. All she has to do is paperwork and answer the phone, if you think she would be interested."

"I think she needs to rest for the next week and get her strength back but if it can wait that long, I'll ask her about it." I told him thoughtfully. "Might give her a bit of independence since she lost her other job. This would be easier on her."

"Sounds like a plan, I'll talk to Fury, Fang and Rider. They will keep an eye on her too. I'm going to head out, got a few things to do. We have a ride tomorrow; I'm guessing you aren't going this time." He said as he put his jacket back on.

"Nah, I'd love to, but I need to stick around here for now. Keep an eye on the Annie situation. Make sure she is eating and taking care of herself. Thanks for picking up the groceries for me." I walked him to the door and patted him on the back. "Call me when you get back."

"Will do, you should reach out to Lucy and see if she would bring Sarah over for a visit. Might be good for Annie to see you interact with her." He suggested as he got in his truck to drive to his place behind the clubhouse. I closed the door and considered that for a minute. It might be good for her to have a female friend too. Lucy lived in Freedom with Stone, but it wasn't that far away.

Since Annie was napping, I decided to workout. I had a small gym in the garage of my house. I set up half of it as a workout space. I liked to stay in shape. Changing into some sweats and a tank I headed out there. I was so engrossed in my workout with my music playing loudly in the background that I didn't hear Annie come out. I was doing my pull ups when I saw her out of the corner of my eye. I did my last four and then dropped to the mat under me. I turned to face her and grabbed a towel to pat myself down. She let her gaze roam over me, and I felt myself harden in my sweats. Damn the little vixen was getting to me. Even being six months pregnant wasn't a turn-off. She was beautiful and I just knew with some more rest and nourishment she would be even more stunning.

"What's up darlin'?" I asked as I headed toward her. She bit her lip and swallowed hard looking down.

"I fixed us some sandwiches for lunch." She told me as she turned away and walked into the house. I saw her sit down at the table with her food and some milk. She was squirming in her seat and squeezing her legs together. I narrowed my brows watching her.

"I need a quick shower; I'll be out in five minutes to eat with you." I told her as I headed to the bathroom. I stripped as soon as I closed the door turning the water on. Hell, I should probably take a cold shower. I scrubbed off and washed my hair quickly. Toweling off, I realized I forgot to bring clothes in the bathroom. I saw my robe hanging on the rack and put it on. Walking to my room I threw on a pair of jeans and a shirt and went to eat with her. She was sitting there nibbling on a piece of bread slowly.

"Are you able to eat that or do you need something else?" I asked and she jumped. She didn't hear me come in since she was clearly lost in her thoughts. "I'm sorry, I should learn to make noise."

"It's okay and yes, I just wanted to start slowly to make sure it wouldn't disagree with me. I made you pastrami, beef and provolone. Mine is just turkey and provolone. I wanted to keep it as bland as possible for now. I also have some plain chips and the salt seems to be settling my tummy okay." She told me as she slipped a couple of chips in her mouth and moaned. Damnit there it went again. I was walking around with a Perma hardon around her. No wonder I went home with her if this was the way I was reacting to her. I took a bite of my sandwich, and it was perfect. She had put some brown mustard on the hoagie roll. There was extra meat on it too. I slipped some of the chips onto my plate and took a bite of those too.

"Thank you for fixing lunch. This is good." I glanced up and she just shrugged. I didn't know what to do. I knew I had been pretty mean when she came to my door, and I seemed to be gruff on a good day. I didn't want her to walk on eggshells around me. I heard tapping on the door and heard Doc holler at me. "Come on in Doc."

"I got the results back. I figured you would like them sooner rather than later." Doc walked over and laid the envelope on the table. "Miss Annie, you sure look like are feeling a little better. There is some color in your cheeks."

"Yes Sir, I have actually slept quite a bit and Zeke has been feeding me well." She smiled at him. Doc Torres smiled back at her as he patted her shoulder, I growled. They both looked at me in surprise. "Did you just growl at him?"

Zeke mumbled under his breath and shoved another bite in his mouth. Doc snickered and winked at her. UGH. I snatched the envelope up and opened it. Looking inside I saw what I already knew. I started to hand it to her, and she looked at me with hurt in her eyes, got up and left the room. I watched her head straight to the bathroom.

"You're an idiot. She didn't need to see the test; she knew you were the father." Doc looked at me and said "Look Undertaker, I get that she isn't Lisa. You need to realize that Lisa would come back and kick your ass herself if she saw you throwing away a chance at happiness. You are great with kids, and you are going to be a father. If you don't sort your shit, someone is going to lay claim to that little girl. She is a looker and not everyone has a problem dating a pregnant woman."

"She wouldn't even be pregnant if I hadn't been drunk." I shouted and punched the wall. I heard a gasp and turned to see her standing at the doorway. Her face paled and she ran to the bedroom and slammed the door. "Well fuck."

"You have some groveling to do. If you decide you aren't going to step up, give me a call. I'll take care of her." Doc walked out and slammed the door behind him. I sat down and put my head in my hands. I needed to calm down before trying to talk to her. It took everything in me not to throw something at my friend as he left. I needed to get my shit together. This was happening, I was going to be a father. It's something I always wanted but kept to myself, so I didn't hurt my late wife. I adored Stone and Lucy's daughter Sarah. They brought her to visit regularly. I guess my struggle is mostly with what kind of relationship I want with Annie.

I knew I needed to apologize but I didn't know what the hell to say to her. I knew she went and threw up her lunch. I needed to get some liquids in her. I got up and pulled down a sleeve of crackers and poured her a ginger ale over ice. I knocked on her bedroom door.

"Annie, can I come in?" I asked then I heard it. She was crying. Nope couldn't stand that I tried to open the door, but she had locked it. "Annie let me in."

"Leave me alone." She yelled, I started to walk away but I heard a sob and shook my head. It was an old-fashioned lock, so I just grabbed a screwdriver and unlocked it to open the door. I walked in to find her curled up on the bed with her arms around her knees crying. Her shoulders were shaking. I felt like an ass.

"Ah, hell Annie. I'm sorry you heard that. I didn't mean it like it sounded though." I sat down beside her on the bed and touched her shoulder. She flinched away and refused to look at me. "I lost my wife a few years ago. I had not been with anyone since then. I drank all the time and stayed to myself. I rarely even went riding with the club. The night I was with you I had already been drinking when I got there, and apparently you were the first woman to turn my head since my wife died. I wish I could remember being with you. I was so drunk that when I woke up beside you and couldn't remember what happened I was horrified. You looked so young and innocent there and I decided to go home and sober up. I haven't had a drop of alcohol since that night. I blacked out when I got home. I don't even know how old you are. I do know that I am very attracted to you, and I want to get to know you better."

I handed her some tissue, and she snatched it out of my hand, dabbing at her eyes. She slowly sat up and crossed her legs looking at me. She studied my face for a few minutes as if trying to decide if she believed me.

"You thought I was trying to scam you or push off someone else's baby on you. I'm not a liar and I have never been with another man. I am 28 years old, and I have been on my own for a long time." She told me defensively. "I'm not the most outgoing person and I have been taking care of myself. I don't date and I was never interested in sex until I met you. I had seen you come in a few times with the other guys, you always kept to yourself. That night you showed an interest in me. You were charming, flirty and it was nice. When I got off you were going to walk me to my car and then suddenly you were kissing me, and I didn't want you to stop. We ended up back at my place and well you know what happened even if you don't remember it. I woke up the next morning and you were just gone. No note, nothing to show you were there. I was a little hurt and very embarrassed but I'm a big girl, so I decided to just go on about my business. A few months later I started getting sick over certain smells and couldn't keep anything down. I started losing sleep, losing weight but my clothes were not fitting right. I was so tired that I forgot orders and ran to the bathroom so much that I got fired. I had my rent paid up for another month so I tried to find something else, but I guess I looked as run down as I felt so no one would hire me. I finally realized that if I didn't get some medical care soon, I would lose the baby. I knew you were with the Ripper's MC, and I knew where the compound was, so I spent the last bit of cash I had on an Uber to get there."

"You did the right thing coming to me. I'm sorry I was such a bastard that night. I'm going to take care of you both." I told her as I lifted her chin to look her in the eyes. "I understand if you don't want anything else to do with me. I would deserve that, but if you are interested and willing, I would really like to get to know you."

She looked up at me with her puffy eyes, her tear-stained cheeks and nodded. Her eyes were fixed on my mouth, so I reached up slowly, cupping the back of her head I kissed her. She froze for a minute before she snaked her arms around my neck and kissed me back. I pulled back gently stroking her cheek and then kissed her forehead.

"Go splash some water on your face and we will see about trying to feed you again." I told her as I left her sitting there staring at me.

7

Annie

I touched my lips and watched him walk out of the room. That sure went differently than I expected. I got up and padded across the hall to the bathroom. I found a washcloth and wiped my face down; my hair was still in a braid, so I left it and went to find Zeke. I knew he went by Undertaker or Taker, but I couldn't call him that. I walked in the kitchen to find him heating up some chicken noodle soup. There was also a loaf of sourdough bread on the counter. That sounded really good. I went to pour myself a glass of water, but he stopped me and fixed it instead.

"Sit down, this will be done soon. I'm also going to fix you a small glass of ginger ale to sip on as well." He told me as he handed me the drinks and then turned back to the stove to stir the soup. "This will be ready in a minute. Do you want your bread toasted in the oven?"

"No thanks, I'm fine with it the way it is." I told him between sips. I watched as he ladled the soup into two deep bowls and then sliced the bread. He carried the bowls to the table and sat the bread in the middle.

"Give it a minute to cool off, don't want you to burn your mouth." He said, handing me a piece of bread. I took a bite, and it was so good I finished the slice before I realized it. He smiled and placed another one in front of me. I took a bite of my soup, and it was delicious. "Did you make this?"

"Yes, I love to cook. It relaxes me." He said smiling at me. Wow, what a smile. Geez, the man was so well built and intense. He made me wet just being around him. He continued eating and I finished my soup and the bread. I was so full, but it felt like it was settling ok on my stomach. I sipped at my ginger ale hoping to keep my meal down.

"Why don't you stay there for a few minutes and prop your feet on the other chair." He suggested as he cleaned up the kitchen. I watched him bustle around the kitchen and the next thing I knew he was carrying me to the couch. I blinked up at him and realized I must have been nodding off.

"I'm sorry, you made us a nice dinner and I fell asleep on you." I said frowning. He started to put me down and I kept my arms around his neck. "Will you sit with me please?" I didn't want him to let go of me. It felt so nice being in his arms.

"I'm glad that you were able to keep the soup down and I would be glad to sit with you." He said as he sat down with me in his lap and pulled a blanket over us. He reached over and handed me the remote. "Find something to watch and we will just relax here for a while."

I took the remote and clicked on Netflix, I found Supernatural and left it on that. Putting the remote down I snuggled into his arms and laid my head against his chest. We sat like that for a few episodes, and I started nodding off again.

"Baby let's get you to bed, you're wiped out. We can watch more tomorrow." He said as he turned off the television and carried me to the bathroom to use the potty and brush my teeth. My eyes were drooping as he helped me out of the sweatpants and tucked me in. It was so nice having someone take care of me. He brushed the hair back from my face and kissed my forehead. He left the bathroom light on, and my door cracked so that it wasn't completely dark. I fell asleep and a few hours later I was freezing, I tried tucking the blankets around me tighter, but I couldn't get warm. Finally, I gave up and went to Zeke's room. He was asleep on the side facing the door. I tiptoed to the other side of the bed and slid in beside him. It was so warm near him. I was still shivering but I felt better already. Suddenly he rolled over and pulled me up against his chest wrapping his arm around my waist. I froze and glanced over my shoulder at him. He looked at me and kissed my nose.

"Go back to sleep baby, I'll keep you warm." He said and he held me to him. I had not felt anything this wonderful since the night our son was conceived. This was so much better though because he was sober, and he wasn't leaving. I snuggled in and fell back to sleep. I woke up the next morning with Zeke still wrapped around me. I really needed to get up. I tried to ease out from under him and his eyes shot open pinning me with his stare. I froze wondering if he forgot I climbed into his bed last night. I felt him slowly relax and a smile played across his handsome face.

"Where you trying to go, angel?" he asked as he kissed my neck and sucked at the spot behind my ear. I moaned and squirmed, it felt so good, but I really had to pee.

"I have to pee." I blushed as I looked at him. He chuckled and let me up. I sprinted to the bathroom, used the potty, brushed my teeth and washed my hands before going back into his bedroom. I stood in the doorway looking at him and was a little embarrassed by everything.

"Thanks for letting me sleep with you last night. I woke up really cold and couldn't get warm. You are always so warm, I thought that would help." I was biting my lip and looking down at my feet. I suddenly saw him in front of me. I looked up and he leaned down and kissed me. He slid his hands down my back and picked me up with his hands under my thighs. Turning around he carried me back to bed.

"I really want to ravish you, but first we need to get some crackers and ginger ale in you before you get sick." He kissed my nose and headed to the kitchen. I could not believe he did that. It was so sweet. I sat there and a few minutes later he came in with a sleeve of crackers and a glass of ginger ale. Sitting them on the nightstand he climbed on the bed with me and pulled me into his lap.

"Ok, have some of this so we can be sure your tummy is settled." He said as he held me close and nuzzled my neck. I ate the crackers and drank the ginger ale with as much haste as I could manage. I wanted him so bad. When I finished, he continued to hold me while kissing my neck and shoulders. When I felt like I was going to be okay I turned around and straddled his lap. I wrapped my arms around his neck and looked at him as I leaned toward his mouth. I noticed he had cleaned up his beard some and it was so hot. I kissed him, he immediately opened his mouth for me to explore with my tongue. He tasted like toothpaste and coffee. He kissed me back, tongue dueling with mine and he sucked my lip into his mouth. Kissing Zeke was a treat in itself. The man had skills, he started to kiss down my neck and behind my ear where I was so sensitive. I moaned as he picked me up and laid me back on the bed. Hovering over me he slid my top off and then started to kiss across my collar bone to my breasts. He paid attention to every noise and whimper to see what I liked the most. Sucking my breast into his mouth he kneaded the other one at the same time. I could feel every lick, suck and nibble in my clit. I was getting restless, and my hands roamed over his back pulling his shirt off. He released my breast long enough to reach behind him with one hand and pulled the shirt off throwing it to the floor. He looked at me and started back down my stomach to my belly button swirling his tongue around and dipping into it. I felt a fresh wash of heat in my core and I knew my thighs were damp from how excited I was. He kissed his way down to my mound using his hands to spread me open for him, I jumped when he swiped his tongue through my folds and sucked my clit into his mouth. He hummed while doing it and I had a death grip on his hair as he proceeded to eat me like I was his favorite dessert. No man had ever done this before, even him. He had been too drunk the first night we were together. He slipped a finger inside me and slowly worked it around before adding a second to stretch me.

"Damn baby, you're so tight. I can't wait to feel you strangle my cock." He groaned as he started to curl his fingers and hit my g-spot triggering the strongest orgasm I had ever felt. I screamed his name at the top of my lungs and my body went limp like a noodle. I looked down at him as he licked his lips and his fingers. God that was so freaking hot. Suddenly he prowled his way back up my body and fit himself to my entrance. Zeke looked me in the eyes and entwined his hands with mine holding them above my head as he slowly slid inside me. It was a tight fit and I was feeling every single inch as he thrust all the way to the hilt. When he was fully seated, he paused, waiting to be sure I was okay. I licked my lips and raised my hips to meet him.

"Please move, I need you so bad." I said in a husky voice, loving the feeling of him against me. It was so intimate with him looking in my eyes as he took me for the second time. This was like a first because he was in the moment this time and fully coherent. There was no doubt he wouldn't forget it this time. He started a rhythm that felt really good, and he would lean in and kiss my lips and neck between thrusts. I wanted to touch him so badly, but he had my hands wrapped in his.

"I want to touch you, Zeke" I moaned as I tried to free my hands.

"Not this time, if you touch me, I will lose it. I want you to come again before I finish." He kept pounding into me until he rubbed his groin against my clit, and I came all over him. He followed a few thrusts after and then gently pulled out of me and rolled to his side. He reached over and pulled me against his chest while we caught our breath. I couldn't believe how amazing it was even with me being so pregnant. This man was twenty years older than me and still WOW!!!!

8

Zeke

I really hated that I could not remember our first time. If it was even a fraction as amazing as this was, I really missed out. I could have had her in my life and in my bed for the last six months, damn. I held her tight against me and didn't want to move. She was curled up to me and her hand was playing on the tattoos on my stomach. She seemed to really like them. As her hand dipped lower my body started responding again and I couldn't believe how quickly I was recovering. She seemed to have a direct line to my cock. Slowly she scooted down so that she was kissing my abdomen and lower until she slid my cock into her hot wet mouth. I gasped at the feel of her suckling me, it felt amazing, and I was pretty sure she had never done this before. She used one hand to stroke what she couldn't fit into her mouth while tonguing and sucking alternately at the crown and swirling her tongue below it. I was going to blow if she didn't stop. I tried to get her to move but she slid her hands under my ass and held on tighter.

"If you don't want to swallow you need to stop." I told her hoarsely. She glanced up at me then sucked harder and I shot down her throat.

She swallowed every drop and then cleaned me up then laid her head on my stomach. "Damn baby, that was so fucking hot."

She just kind of mumbled an "mmmhmmm" and fell asleep. Well hell, she was so cute. Her beautiful hair was spread across my chest and her hands were on either side of me. Her body was between my legs lying over me. I didn't want to move her, but I really needed to go to the bathroom. I sat up a bit and gently eased her to her side and slid out of the bed. She grabbed my pillow and cuddled it. I smiled at her and went to take care of myself. I didn't want to wash off her scent, so I just threw on some clothes and went to start some laundry, leaving her to rest. She still had a lot of sleep to catch up on.

I need to go to work tomorrow. I had taken a few days off to get her settled. I would like to see if she would be interested in the reception job. That would allow me to keep an eye on her, make sure she eats and rests. She would be able to sit for most of it. I pulled out stuff to make pancakes, I mixed the batter and put it in the fridge. I would wait until she woke up to fix them. I checked the fridge and made a list of anything we may need from the store. Leaving the list on the counter so that Annie could add to it. I hear the crunch of gravel and an engine shut off. Walking over to the door I opened it up to see Lucy laughing as she pulled Sarah out. Sarah started running to me.

"Uncle Santa, Uncle Santa, I misses you so much." Sarah says in her little voice. I caught her in my arms and swung her around tickling her just to hear the sweet giggles.

"Hey princess, what are you two lovely ladies doing here?" I asked Lucy as she smirked at me. Oh, someone told her about Annie.

"There is a couple of bags of stuff in the trunk if you wouldn't mind grabbing those. Stone would have a fit if I tried to get them." Lucy said as she walked into the house. "Where is she?"

I followed them inside and touched Lucy's arm, shaking my head holding my finger to my mouth. I pointed to the couch. I went into my room, closing the door behind me and saw Annie standing in my T-shirt, eyes wide as saucers.

"Seems we have company; I didn't know they were coming over but I'm glad. You will like Lucy and Sarah is a little doll." I told her.

"Zeke, I don't have any pants in here." She hissed. I chuckled and went to my drawers pulling out a pair of sweats with a drawstring for her. She took them and slipped them on. I also handed her a pair of socks.

"Come on baby, you look fine." I said as I tugged her out of the bedroom. She walked behind me holding my hand. Sarah spotted her first and squealed running up to us.

"Who is this Uncle Santa?" she bounced. "She is pretty." Sarah was in jeans and one of her princess sweatshirts today with Cinderella boots on to match. She was adorable with her pigtails and big toothy smile.

"Princess Sarah, I'd like you to meet my girlfriend, Annie." I smiled down at her. "Annie, this is my friend Sarah and her mother, Lucy."

Lucy got up from the couch and walked over to shake her hand. Annie's hand squeezed mine then she released me.

"Hi, Annie I'm Lucy, this little imp is my daughter. My husband is working, or he would have come as well." Lucy stuck out her hand to shake with Annie, who took it.

"I'm Marianna Preston, my friends call me Annie." She said, I realized she was shaky due to having not eaten yet.

"Ladies, I was about to make some pancakes. Who's hungry?" I asked, smiling, as Sarah started bouncing.

"Oh goody, Uncle Santa makes the best pancakes." Sarah told Annie who grinned at the nickname. I pulled the batter out of the fridge and started to cook. I scrambled some eggs to go with them and when everything was done, we all sat down for breakfast.

"I'm sorry we barged in on you today, I just wanted to bring you some things to make you more comfortable and offer to take you shopping one evening." Lucy said as she nibbled at her food. Annie was surprised, she wasn't used to so much kindness.

"Thank you, I would love to, but I have to find a job first." Annie frowned as she ate her breakfast. Lucy looked at me and raised her eyebrows.

"When Axle came by, he mentioned us needing a new receptionist at the shop. Our last one quit and moved back home. I was going to see if you were interested. The pay is good, we also provide health insurance. You would be sitting mostly so it's something that won't be hard on you." I looked up to see her smiling at me.

"You won't get sick of me being around?" she asked me, biting her lip. "If you're sure then yes, I would love to."

"Good, you can go with me tomorrow." I said as I cleaned up our dishes. Sarah was a sticky mess, so I dampened a paper towel and wiped off her little face and hands. I heard a gasp and looked up to see Annie watching me with a look of surprise on her face.

"Annie, let's take the bags into the bedroom and I'll show you what I brought while the Undertaker has kid duty." Lucy got up and started to get a bag when Zeke took them, shaking his head and put them in the bedroom for us. "Thank you."

"No problem, princess and I will watch cartoons." He said as he scooped Sarah up and put her on his lap handing her the remote.

9

Annie

Lucy followed me into the bedroom and closed the door. She started to dump the bags on the bed. I watched as she pulled out several maternity outfits. I was feeling very overwhelmed at the moment.

"I'm sorry we barged in like this. I heard about you and was just so happy to see him with someone finally." Lucy explained looking sheepish. "I know he looks rough and mean but that man is a marshmallow when it comes to women and children. My Sarah adores him."

"I can see that. You're right, he really does have a soft side to him. I'm still getting to know him. I'm embarrassed to admit that this was the result of a one night stand he doesn't even remember." I rubbed my belly blushing. "He knows the baby is his now, but this has been a little awkward for us both."

"Look Annie, I don't know the details of your relationship with the Undertaker. What I know is that he wanted you to have some things to wear to make you comfortable so he could take you shopping for whatever you need. He has had a hard go of it the last few years and the guys told me you are the first woman he has shown any interest in drunk or sober." Lucy looked me in the eye and handed me an outfit. "Now let's see what fits."

We talked while I tried on several outfits, finding several that fit me. It was nice having clothes that were not from a thrift store. I settled on a pair of stretch jeans and a long-sleeved flannel top. I put away the things that fit me and the things that didn't she was taking back with her. We walked into the living room to find Sarah snuggled up in Zeke's lap sound asleep. My heart melted at the sight. I knew right then he was going to be an amazing father to our son. He looked up at us and met my eyes and smiled. I was a goner. I sat down beside him on the couch and gently brushed her hair off of her face. She was so sweet and clearly adored him. Lucy collected her things and Zeke carried Sarah out to her car and buckled her into her booster seat. After they left, we came back inside the house, and I threw my arms around him.

"Whoa, what's this about?" chuckling, he hugged me close. "I'll take it any way I can get it."

"You are so wonderful. First you save me from being raped, then you take care of me, now I have a job and a new friend." I babbled as I buried my face in his chest. Zeke led me to the couch and sat down pulling me into his lap.

"So, you don't mind working with me?" he asked me, looking at my face. I looked into his dark brown eyes like melted dark chocolate and kissed him. Suddenly all I wanted was to strip him naked and worship his hard body. I wanted to explore his tattoos and those ripped abs showing him how much I desired him. "I'll take that as a no."

He stood up with me in his arms and walked us to the bedroom. In no time he had stripped us both naked and was inside me. I moaned at the feel of him stretching me and kissing my neck. I didn't think I would ever get tired of the way he makes me feel. This time was fast because we were both so worked up and I was so turned on I didn't need any foreplay. As he held my hip in one hand and my leg up by his neck with the other, he moved faster and faster. I could tell when he was close by the look on his face and the tension in his body. He released my leg and reached down to play with my clit until I was flying with him. After he caught his breath, he gently arranged me on his chest and played with my hair.

"We need to go to the store. I want to be sure you have what you need as far as clothing, shoes etc. so you will be ready for work tomorrow. Nothing fancy needed, just comfortable clothes, jeans, t-shirts, hoodies, whatever. We had a late breakfast so we could get lunch while we're out." I nodded as I wasn't feeling very verbal at the moment. I was still recovering from the orgasm and great sex we just had. I could not get over how fast everything was going between us.

"Did you mean it about getting to know each other and trying to make this work with us?" I asked, afraid to look at him. He raised up a little in the bed pulling me with him then lifted my chin to look into my eyes.

"Baby, I have not felt anything like this for another woman since my wife died. You make this old man feel alive again and excited for the future. So yes, I want to explore a relationship with you besides being your baby's father. I like you a lot." He searched my face for any sign of panic, but I felt a strange sense of calm about everything.

"Okay, I want that too. I know I'm a lot younger and I don't want you to get bored with me. I'm a hard worker and I'm usually very independent." I confessed as I bit my lip looking at him. "I am very excited to have a job, especially one that doesn't involve me on my feet all day long."

"Good, let's run through the shower and get dressed. We have a lot to do today then I want to feed you and let you get a nap later." He said as he slapped my ass and got up. Laughing we took our shower and got dressed again. I slipped on the sneakers that Lucy brought me, slipping my ID into my pocket. I didn't have a purse; I had no phone or anything to put in one. Zeke noticed this and frowned.

The drive to town wasn't bad, we pulled up to a Walmart and got out. I planned to pay him back for whatever he bought me today. I didn't say anything because I knew he would just scowl and grumble. Smiling to myself I took his hand when he offered it, and we started looking through the store. There wasn't much of a maternity area, but I found some stretchy jeans and some yoga pants that would last a while as well as plenty of tops. I picked out some bras and panties as well. A pack of socks and he led me to the coats. After outfitting me with a new wardrobe we went and picked up toiletry items that I needed as well. I was picking up a backpack style purse when I saw a woman walk up and put her arms around Zeke.

"Hey Undertaker, haven't seen you around the club in a while?" the busty blonde said as she dragged her long red nail down his chest.

"Dawn, I haven't been to the club in months. I don't do that anymore. If you will excuse us, my girlfriend and I are shopping." He said as he wrapped his arm around me and pulled me close to him. She looked me up and down and sneered at me.

"You are planning on raising some other man's brat?" she asked him with a smirk. I was really not liking this bitch. Zeke started to defend me when I placed my hand on his chest and shook my head.

"He is the father of our unborn son, so how about you take your trashy ass back to the strip club where you belong, we will go home, and I'll take care of my man's needs." I said calmly and turned us both to the basket and walked away from her. As we reached the checkout counter, I looked up to see Zeke smiling at me.

"What?" I asked blushing. "You didn't think I could handle the trash?"

"Honestly, I wasn't sure what your reaction was going to be. I gotta tell you that the one you had turns me on though. I'm ready to get you home and show you how much I enjoyed it." He whispered in my ear as he slipped the cashier his card. "Let's load up and go home. We can grab some food on the way."

He took my hand and pushed the cart with the other one. We made it home in record time and before we even put up the groceries, he had me bent over the couch with my pants down and he was fucking me hard. Kissing my neck and murmuring dirty stuff in my ear while he reached around and played with my clit until we were both coming. When he pulled out, he patted my back and told me not to move yet. He came back with a damp cloth to clean me up. Then smacked my ass.

"Let's get these groceries and clothes put up." He laughed at the expression on my face. I loved to see him laugh, it made him look younger and more carefree. My goal was to get him to do it as often as possible.

10

Annie

The next morning, we got up, had breakfast and headed to the garage. He told me that everyone there referred to him as Undertaker or just Taker. He said I could just refer to him as Taker to the guys and Zeke was just for us. Axle was there when we arrived, along with a few other guys.

"Hey guys come here a minute." He hollered at them over the noise of the engines and radio. They looked up at us curiously and walked over. "I want you to meet Annie. She is going to be working the desk for us. You are to treat her like she is my old lady."

I looked up at him in surprise. I knew that old lady was the same as wife to bikers. This was him claiming me and I was all melty inside now. Smiling, I looked back as they started making introductions.

"Nice to meet you Annie, I'm Rider. You need anything you let me know." Rider, one of bald guys with a clover tat on one arm and some Chinese lettering on the other. He had a goatee and fierce eyes, but they were smiling right now.

"I'm Fury, anyone breathes in your direction let me know, I'll end them. After I make them suffer of course." This guy was tall, cut with beautiful tats covering his arms. He was beautiful but in a fierce way. Very good looking with dimples. I got the feeling he was serious about his offer though. I shook their hands and then looked over at Axle.

"Nice to see you again Annie. You look like you're feeling better." Axle was a looker too, he had black hair with a goatee look and chiseled jaw, I didn't see any tattoos on him but then he was wearing a t-shirt. He seemed close to Zeke, so I wanted him to like me.

Zeke wrapped his arms around me from behind and I leaned my head against him. It felt a little tense, so I figured I'd say something to lighten the mood.

"Geez, do you only let hot guys in the club?" Annie asked. "I mean seriously, there's not an ugly one here." Zeke growled in my ear.

"You don't need to be thinking of anyone else as hot here." he demanded as he tightened his hold on me. I snickered at his possessiveness. "Let's show you what you'll be doing."

The guys laughed at him and went back to work. Axle followed us over to the front desk. Which was a tall counter with a barstool that thankfully had a back on it. I looked at it and back at him raising an eyebrow. I'm a short girl and I'm also going to be getting bigger which could make this set up tricky in a month or two. The guys looked confused for a minute until I tried to get on the barstool.

"Well shit, didn't think about that. Axle, go grab that little step stool and bring it back here. She is going to need it for a few months." He said as he picked me up and sat me on the stool. Then leaned in and kissed me. "Sorry babe, we will get you all fixed up."

Standing behind me, he started showing me the system. It was easy enough to figure out and they only had one line, so the phone was a no brainer. He showed me the online catalogs for parts and a few of the paper ones under the counter. It didn't seem too difficult to learn, mostly learning about the parts and knowing the right questions to ask. I was good with numbers, so I also offered to help with the accounting side. He told me that Gears did the payroll and taxes but if I wanted to help with the billing and deposits that would help a lot. Axle came back out with a small stool and put it under the desk so I could use it when needed. Zeke made sure I had a snack and a large water bottle beside me before he headed into one of the bays to work.

The day went by quickly and I found I enjoyed the work as well as the atmosphere in the shop. The guys were hard workers but very laid back. They worked hard, chattered amongst themselves and blared Metallica, Ozzy and AC/DC in the background. I was pretty sure I was going to love working here. I also had the bonus of seeing my guy all day working bent over an engine. Yummy.

I looked back at the computer and got wrapped up in getting tickets ready and lost track of time. I almost jumped out of my skin when I felt Zeke's lips on my shoulder.

"Hey babe, you ready to grab some lunch?" he asked as he turned me around to face him. He had pulled off his coveralls, so he was back to his jeans and t-shirt. I licked my lips as I looked at him and suddenly found myself in his arms heading to the back office. He closed and locked the door and then sat on the couch with me in his lap. He was kissing me and had his hands under my shirt. I moaned and he leaned back and looked at me with hunger in his eyes. I seemed to stay turned on around him, so I ground myself against his hard cock and leaned down to suck on his neck. I wanted to mark him and show everyone he was mine. He stood me up and pulled my pants down then unbuttoned his jeans and slid himself out. He turned me facing away and then settled me on his cock entering me in one thrust. I moaned again. I couldn't help it, he felt so good. He held me around the waist and thrust into me while holding me with my back against his chest. He sucked on my neck and kissed it and my shoulder. He adjusted and started grazing my g-spot as he pulled out and back in. Suddenly I shouted and came hard. He held me to him for a minute, then reached over for some tissue to clean us up.

"That was amazing, but I still need to feed you." He chuckled. He put himself back in his pants and buttoned them back up and then helped me pull mine back up. "What do you want for lunch?"

"I want some chicken tenders and fries with ranch dressing." I told him as my stomach growled. He smiled and helped me up. We left the office, and the guys gave a few whistles and cat calls. My face turned beet red, and Zeke gave them a wink. I hid my face on his shoulder as we walked out to go to the diner across the street. He held my hand and slid into a booth beside me. When the waitress came over to take our order, she added an extra bounce to her step upon seeing Zeke. UGH these women I swear.

"Well, hello Sugar, what can I get for you and your daughter?" she said licking her lips as she stared at my man's chest. Stupid assumption anyway considering he was sitting beside me with his hand on my thigh. Obviously, a possessive gesture not a fatherly one.

"This is my old lady and the mother of my child. Now I'll have the steak medium rare with a loaded baked potato and she wants your chicken tender platter with fries and plenty of ranch dressing on the side. We would both like some water and a glass of chocolate milk." He said pulled me tighter against him. I reached up and pulled my hair to the other side so she could see the huge hickey he had given me right before we got here.

"I'll get your order in and bring your drinks right back." She had the grace to look embarrassed as she walked away. Zeke reached up and turned my face to him and kissed me.

"Does it bother you that people might think I'm your father?" he asked, looking me in the eye. I could see the vulnerability in his gaze. I could tell he was honestly concerned about my answer.

"Honey, you don't give me fatherly feels at all and I don't care what people think. They don't know us or anything about our relationship. If it doesn't bother you, it doesn't bother me." I said as I hugged him and kissed his cheek. The waitress brought our drinks out and scowled at me as she put the chocolate milk in front of me. Taking a drink, I looked around and saw a couple of stares but overall, not too bad.

"I have lived here a long time. I eat here several times a week and they haven't seen me with a woman since my wife died years ago. So, some are just surprised." He said as the waitress came back with our orders. I dug into my food, suddenly starving, everything was delicious. "Slow down baby, don't want you to get sick."

"It's really good and I was so hungry. Your boy is taking it out of me." I winked at him. He beamed when I said, 'his boy'. This kid was going to be spoiled rotten. "What are we going to call him?"

"What about Matthew for his first name?" he suggested. "It was my father's name."

"Matthew Zeke Richards, has a nice ring to it." I said as his eyes widened. "What honey?"

"You want him to have my name?" he asked. "I mean obviously he will have my last name; I just didn't know you were thinking of my first name too."

"I think it's perfect and since you said you aren't going anywhere, and we seem to be together now it seemed like a good idea." I was suddenly nervous, and my stomach lurched as I looked up at him.

"There is no seeming, we are together, and I am honored you want to name our son after me." he said as his eyes glistened. "Eat up we need to get back."

"I'm going to get it to go, and I can snack on it. It's too much to eat at once." I told him. I pointed to the plate and got the waitress' attention. She brought a takeout container and a cup to put my drink in. "I'm ready." He helped me up and we went back to work.

11

Zeke

We slid into a comfortable routine over the last month. Sharing the cooking and cleaning around the house. I started clearing out the guestroom for a nursery while she slept. I planned to take her away for the weekend. While we were gone Blade and Axle were going to paint the nursery and help assemble the furniture. When we got back, I would take her to pick out the bedding and décor for the room. I felt like this would show her how serious I was about having them with me.

Annie and I had more in common than I would have originally thought. We liked a lot of the same shows, music, foods. She also had a thing for classic cars and wanted to ride on the back of my bike so bad she couldn't stand it. I told her as soon as the baby is here, and she is healed we will make that happen. We were going to leave a little early, so I called and had our lunch delivered. I was taking it back to the office when she came out of the restroom. Her hand on her stomach smiling ear to ear.

"What are you grinning at baby?" I asked her as she grabbed my hand and put it on her belly. I felt a roll and a kick. "Whoa is that, Mattie?" She grinned at me and nodded.

"He has been kicking and moving up a storm today." She said as she held my hand on her belly and looked at me. I looked up at her beautiful face and realized I had fallen in love with this woman. She was giving me a precious gift I thought I'd never have. She has seamlessly blended into my life, and I love it. I couldn't wait to spend the weekend alone with her and then see her face when we got home.

"I ordered you lunch, I got you a crispy chicken salad with ranch and a side order of garlic bread. Eat up you're going to need your energy tonight." I winked at her and pulled out my burger and fries. We ate quickly and got back to work. I told Axle we were leaving at three today. We were pretty well caught up and having her work at the desk has been a huge help. At three I went and stripped off my coveralls, washed my hands, then collected our coats. We had a bag in the truck.

She closed down the computer and came over for me to put her coat on. I loved that she let me take care of her like that. She was fiercely independent but at the same time enjoyed my protective nature. Probably since she had not experienced it in a long time.

"You two have fun, enjoy your weekend." Axle shouted from under the car he was working on. Fury just jerked his chin in our direction as he continued his custom paint job on the motorcycle he was working on.

"Let's go we have a couple of hours drive ahead of us." I said as I buckled her in and went around to the driver's side. We headed out and I noticed she was very quiet. I glanced over and she had curled her arm up and was asleep against the window. Poor baby, she was getting tired more often lately. I had been having her take naps in the office. Keeping a pillow and blanket in there for her. She insisted on continuing to work so I made sure she took care of herself while doing it. I also loved having her there where I could keep an eye on her.

We arrived at the cabin I rented about six, she stirred when she felt us stop and the engine cut off. She blinked and looked over at me blushing.

"Sorry, I fell asleep on you." She said as she unbuckled her seatbelt. I leaned over and kissed her.

"You needed the rest baby." I said as I got out and went to open her door. I threw our bag over my shoulder and helped her out of the truck. She stopped and looked around, her eyes bright and a flush on her cheeks from the cold wind. She was beautiful.

"Wow Zeke, this place is beautiful. I mean I love your house too, but this just looks so peaceful." She wanted to look around more, but it was cold and dark.

"Let's go in and I'll start a fire so we can warm up. I had groceries delivered for the weekend. It won't take long to throw something together." We walked inside and the place really was charming. It was log cabin style inside with a deep leather sofa in front of the fireplace, a couple of arm chairs and there was a small table in the kitchen next to a picture window. There was only one bedroom and there was also a huge clawfoot tub in the bathroom beside the shower. I saw her shivering and wrapped my arms around her from behind.

"It's so cold in here, but it looks so cozy." Annie leaned back against my chest. "I will go find some hot chocolate to make and see what we can throw together for dinner while you start the fire." Turning in my arms she put her hands on my face pulling it down to her and she kissed me sweetly. The expression on her face made me choke up. I kissed her back and then hugged her to me.

"I'll get you warm soon love." I told her as I set up the logs in the fireplace and started it. She found some hot chocolate packets and was boiling water to make it. I saw there were already prepared meals in the fridge. Some stew, lasagna and a few other things. I pulled out the stew and dumped it into a pot, adding just a bit of water and turned on the stove to heat it. There was a fresh loaf of sourdough bread on the counter, so I sliced some of that to go along with it. We sat down the eat dinner. The room was starting to warm up some so I slipped off my coat. The stew was good and filling. I was pleased to see she had a good appetite. We ate in silence and just enjoyed each other's company. I loved that she didn't feel the need to fill the silence with meaningless chatter. She was very mature, smart, funny and I was crazy about her. I still had a little guilt creep up occasionally, but I reminded myself that Lisa would want me to move on and be happy. She would be thrilled that I got to be a father. After we finished eating, I told her to enjoy her hot chocolate and I cleaned up the dishes. After adding more logs to the fire, I led her into the bedroom. It was warming up throughout the cabin, so I walked her over to the bed and started kissing her as I stripped her clothes off. I was sliding her hoodie off along with the shirt under it. She was pulling at my shirt so I leaned forward so she could pull it over my head. I loved how she reacted to my body. It was good to know she found me attractive. We started kissing again and I released her bra and kissed down to her breasts taking them in my mouth in turns suckling at them. They had grown over the last month as they prepared to feed our son. Her body was still beautiful even growing. I had started rubbing cocoa butter on her belly every night and talking to the baby. She held my head to her breasts and moaned. Her legs trembling, I turned her around and she sat on the edge of the bed. I stripped out of my shoes socks and pants kneeling before her. I pulled her jogging pants off along with her underwear. Kissing my way down to her belly I placed kisses over it then down to her mound. Her scent was intoxicating, and I dove in with my tongue. She screamed as I sucked her clit, and she came all over my mouth. She had been way more sensitive the last few weeks and I loved it. I continued until I pushed her into another orgasm, then I fit myself to her entrance and thrust into her. I leaned down kissing her while I moved in and out. She sucked on my tongue and nibbled on my lower lip. She ran her hands down my back to my ass and squeezed. I started to move faster, and I felt her clinch up and then she was pulsing around me as she came again. I followed her shortly after and then rolled us, so I was on my back, and she was curled up to me. I spotted the tissue beside the bed and cleaned us up a bit. I eased out of the bed and walked into the bathroom to run a bath. I found some bath salts in the cabinet and poured a generous amount in, then went to collect my girl. Picking her up I carried her into the bathroom and turned off the water before stepping into the tub and settling her in front of me. She sighed and leaned back against me. I picked up the washcloth and put some bath gel on it to start washing her. She was dozing in my arms completely relaxed.

"Baby, are you still awake?" I whispered in her ear. She nodded as I slipped my hand lower. I washed her thoroughly and had her sit up so I could get her back too. "I love you, Annie."

She turned in my arms and looked at my face in surprise. Her eyes were misty, and she leaned over and kissed me. "I love you too, Zeke." She straddled my lap and sank down on my cock slowly. I let her set the pace since I knew that this position had me deeper. She worked herself up and down my cock as I suckled her breasts with my mouth and tongue. She was so beautiful caught up in her pleasure I reached between us and played with her clit. She picked up speed and suddenly arched back and screamed my name as she came. I grabbed her hips and thrust a few more times before I joined her. I nudged her on her knees so I could clean her up again and then pulled the plug. I got out patting dry and then grabbed a towel and lifted her out. After drying her off we went and climbed into the bed. I pulled her close to me and held her tight.

12

Annie

I woke up with Zeke's arm thrown over me and his morning erection pressed against my ass. He was still asleep. I could feel the even breathing in my hair. He liked to sleep with me wrapped up in his arms tight. I loved it, I felt safe in his arms. I really needed to go to the bathroom, but I just didn't want to move. I felt so happy this morning. We had told each other how we felt last night. I couldn't believe this amazing man was in love with me. How did I get so lucky? Finally, Mattie bouncing on my bladder won and I had to ease out of the bed. I was finishing up and washing my hands when Zeke stumbled into the bathroom. I quickly brushed my teeth while he used the restroom and then went back to the bedroom. I slipped on some fuzzy pajama pants and his hoodie he wore yesterday. I loved wearing them after him because they smelled like his cologne. Slipping on some fuzzy socks I wandered into the living room and saw the fire was low, so I started to put another log on when Zeke took it out of my hand and set me away from the fire. He built it back up and then wrapped me in a blanket depositing me on the couch. Kissing me on the head he went back to adding logs to the fire and then headed to the kitchen.

"You stay warm and I'm going to fix us some coffee and breakfast." He told me as he started the coffee pot and pulled out some ham eggs and hashbrowns. My nausea had finally left around the middle of last month, so I was feeling a lot better and keeping my food down. I watched as he cooked breakfast in his jeans and no shirt looking hot as hell. Good grief my pregnancy hormones had me horny like all the time!!!

"Marianna Leah Preston, if you don't stop looking at me like that, I'm going to spread you on this table and have you for breakfast." He told me in that gravelly voice of his. My eyes widened and I thought about what he said. I got up and walked over to him, reaching around, I turned off the ham and put it on the back burner. He had not started the eggs or hashbrowns yet. I pulled him over to a chair, unbuttoned his jeans and nudged them off. I then dropped a pillow at his feet and knelt in front of him. Licking down his chest and abs I nipped at his hip bone, and he moaned fisting my hair in his hands. I looked up at him as I took his cock into my mouth and took him down to where I almost gagged on him. His eyes flared and he started to pick me up but I released his cock and shook my head.

"No, it's my turn to play." I said as I engulfed him in my mouth again and started working him in and out of my mouth, licking and sucking him. I loved his smell, and he was telling me how good it felt to have me suck him which was making me very wet. I love his filthy mouth talking dirty to me while we had sex. It turned me on so much to hear how much he enjoyed my body, and I certainly was enjoying his too. You would never know this man was almost 50 by his body. If he shaved the beard off, he would likely look about 15 years younger. Might have to see that, all though I don't want the women looking too closely at what was mine. His hands in my hair felt good as he started fucking my mouth. He was close, I could tell by the tightening of his abdomen and his raspy breathing. Suddenly he filled my mouth, and I swallowed down all he offered before raising up and licking my lips.

"Damn baby, just damn." He said as he pulled me into his lap and held me close. "That was amazing. You have to let me catch my breath and then I'll finish breakfast."

I just wrapped my arms around his neck and laid my head on his shoulder. He reached down and slipped his fingers into the sweatpants and felt how wet I was. He rubbed my clit and I moaned into his neck and then he slipped a finger in me and started to finger me while rubbing my clit until I came all over his hand. He pulled it out and licked his fingers clean making me blush again. He winked at me and then stood up and put me down in the chair.

"Behave I need to feed you." He turned back to the stove and finished breakfast while I sat in my post orgasm blissful state. Breakfast was delicious as usual. I could not wait to cook something for him. He was always feeding me and looking after me. It was very sweet. We got dressed and went outside to walk down by the creek. I just wanted some fresh air and to see the property in the daylight. It was beautiful up here.

"Thank you for bringing me here. This is gorgeous and I like having you to myself." I said as we stood looking out from the back porch with his arms around me and a blanket around us. He pulled me back to the swing on the porch and sat down pulling me into his lap.

"I'm sorry I was so hateful when you came to the house. I hate that I said those things to you, and I can't take them back. I really don't remember most of that night. I probably hate that more than you do. I haven't had a drop of alcohol since then. I just got wrapped up in my grief and let it control me. I had some sober days too, but when I did drink it was bad." he said quietly while looking at the water. "You have been a revelation to me. You match my attitude, my sex drive, my humor. It's like you were a piece of me I didn't even know I was missing. I know we haven't really known each other very long but I want the rest of my tomorrows with you."

Listening to what he was saying I glanced up at his handsome face to see he was looking down at me. I never thought I would have someone to look at me like that. I reached up and touched his face and he kissed my hand.

"I didn't know what to think of you. You would come in with your friends and you would stay in the back drinking whiskey. You looked mean and gruff. I didn't have the nerve to talk to you. Then the night we met and created Mattie, you came in and you were friendly, flirting with me. You were so charming. I was attracted to you instantly, and I had not been really attracted to a man ever. I had spent so much time taking care of myself that I had never really dated or shown any interest in guys. I didn't realize how much you had apparently been drinking before you came into Jakes'. When you walked me to my car after my shift and kissed me, I lost control. I suddenly didn't want to be a virgin anymore and I knew I wanted you to be my first. I won't say it was magical. It wasn't, but you did make it good for me. When I woke up and you were gone without a trace of being there, I was suddenly ashamed and embarrassed by my behavior. I was relieved that you stopped coming to the bar, only I thought you had stopped because you didn't want to see me. I didn't know it was because you were getting sober and didn't even remember me." I wrapped my arms around myself as I remembered how used I had felt the next morning.

"Baby, I'm so sorry. I can't even say that I would trade that night because that's why I have you now." He said as he pulled me back to him. "I brought you here for a reason." I watched him get up and kneel in front of me. He reached into his jeans and pulled out a ring.

"I know we haven't been together for long, but I'm in love for the last time in my life. You are it for me and I want to raise our little family together. Marianna Leah Preston will you be my wife, my old lady, my forever girl?" he asked me with a hopeful expression on his handsome face. I blinked, I looked at him and nodded my head.

"YES!!! I will absolutely be your wife." I threw my arms around him, and he chuckled.

"Don't you even want to see the ring?" he asked me as he slid it on my finger. I looked down to see a blue diamond surrounded by white diamonds on a white gold band. It was beautiful. "I wanted something to match your eyes. They are the most beautiful blue I have ever seen."

"Mr. Richards, I'm going to need you to take me to bed now." I said as I winked at him and walked through the back door, I started stripping as I walked towards the fireplace, there was a bearskin rug in front, and I laid down on it waiting for him. I don't know how I went from being a lonely waitress to happy engaged lady with a baby on the way and a job I really enjoy. I just know that I intend to enjoy every single minute I have with this incredible man of mine.

13

Zeke

I followed Annie into the living room watching her strip and followed suit. When I got to where she was displayed on the rug by firelight I was mesmerized by her beauty. Her hair glowed in the light, her eyes were sparkling, skin glowing with her pregnancy and the beautiful roundness that was carrying my son, her legs were shapely, and her little toenails had been painted red. I stood and just drank in the sight of her knowing she was mine. She smiled up at me and held out her hand. Taking it, I knelt down on the rug and made love to my girl. I didn't know how I got this lucky but I was going to cherish her and our son.

The rest of the weekend was spent in bed with the exception of meals, and we napped in between. It was so peaceful. We would have to do this more often. I wanted to marry her before the baby came but I figured I would ask what she wanted when we got home. As we threw our stuff in the bag and left the cabin, I pulled her to the middle of the truck and buckled her in so I could hold her hand comfortably and feel her next to me on the drive home. When we arrived at the house, I saw the light on in the front bedroom that was going to be the nursery. That was their way of letting me know it was done. I parked the truck, collected our bag and held the door for her to get out. We walked into the house, and she started to head to the bathroom. I looked and thankfully the nursery door was closed.

After she came out of the bathroom, she started to go into our bedroom, but I stopped her. I tugged on her hand and smiled at her. I stopped her in front of the other bedroom door.

"Open it." I told her smiling. She looked at me confused, turned the knob and pushed open the door. The bedroom was painted duck egg blue with an oak crib on one wall and a changing table with a rocking chair. There was a chest of drawers as well. She looked at me and then looked back in the room and walked around looking at the furniture, touching everything. I heard a sob and ran over to her pulling her into my arms.

"I'm sorry, is it all wrong, do you hate it?" I asked her as she started giggling through the tears.

"It's perfect, I can't believe you did all this." She said as she smiled at me. I felt relieved and hugged her to me.

"Well actually Axle and Blade did it. That's part of why we went away. I didn't want you around the paint fumes and I also wanted it to be a surprise." I told her as she leaned back against me and held my hands to her belly. Mattie was kicking up a storm. "He sure is active today."

I could not believe the changes in her body over the last six weeks, she was growing and looking healthy. She was glowing and beautiful. I took her hand and walked over to the rocking chair sitting down and pulling her onto my lap.

"You need to decide what kind of bedding and decorations you want for the nursery. We can go look after work tomorrow if you like or you can order the stuff online." I was holding my happiness in my hands right now.

"This is so perfect; I was thinking about 'Cars' the Disney movie. It would be so cute and not so babyish so he can enjoy it longer." She was biting her lip again, so I knew she had something on her mind.

"What are you thinking about baby?" I wanted to know what was causing her to tense up and look nervous.

"I don't want a big wedding. I don't have any family and I just want to be your wife." She said as she plays with my beard. "I'm trying to say I don't want to wait, and I don't want anything fancy."

"Baby, you have my friends and family now too. I would love to take you one day next week and tie the knot. You just pick a day and I'll get us a couple of witnesses." I looked at her and still could not believe she wanted to be with me. My phone vibrated and I pulled it out of my pocket. It was Axle checking to see how she liked the surprise. I handed her the phone, and she typed in a thank you with some cute little emoji's. "Yep, I'm going to see if Lucy wants to stand up with you and I'll have Axle with me. I'm going to aim for Friday."

"Sounds perfect, now feed me I'm starving." I told her. She laughed as she got up and headed toward the kitchen. I followed her and sat down at the counter. She had already pulled out some butter, cheese and bread. Looked like she wanted some grilled cheese sandwiches. "I'll make these and some tomato soup to go with it. Is that okay?"

"Sure, I can cook if you want." I suggested as I watched her. I liked seeing her in my kitchen cooking though. She just seemed so at home here now and I loved it.

"I got it, you sit there and relax." She opened the can of soup and added some milk to it then set it to warm up while she fixed the sandwiches. When it was finished, we sat at the table to eat. "I wanted to cook for you for a change. You're always taking care of me."

"I like taking care of you, it's my job as your man." I told her as I touched her cheek. She smiled across the table at me. "I got the dishes; you go get ready for bed baby."

I cleaned up the kitchen and then went to start a load of laundry, when I walked into our bedroom, I found Annie lying in bed completely naked but asleep. I couldn't help but smile. She must have wanted to play but was so tired she crashed. I leaned over and kissed her nudging her over so I could get her under the covers. She barely stirred as I settled her under the blankets. I stripped down and crawled into bed then pulled her into my arms. I was going to have my hands full with her. I lay there wondering what our son would look like when he arrived. Would he have her hair and eyes or mine, maybe a bit of each. I smiled as I thought about it and imagined her holding our baby to her breast to nurse. This little slip of a woman came crashing into my life and gave me something to live for again. I held her tight while I waited for sleep to take me.

14

Annie

I was wrapped up in an order for the shop, trying to make sure that I didn't miss anything and almost didn't hear her approach my desk.

"Hey Annie." Lucy said smiling. She was alone this time and I smiled back at her. "We need to take you to get a dress for Friday."

"Give me a few more minutes and I'll be ready for my break." I told her as I finished placing the parts order. Suddenly I felt Zeke's arms around me, and I was lifted from the stool.

"You are done for the day. Have fun shopping, I'll see you at home." He said as he kisses me senseless and then slipped his credit card in my hand. "No arguments, go get what you need."

I watched him walk back to the bay area and Lucy was snickering at me. I grabbed my coat and purse then followed her out. Fury was outside on his bike, he looked up and smiled at us.

"You ladies be careful; Annie don't overdo it." He said as he went inside the shop. I just stood there with my mouth open shocked.

"They are all a bit bossy, but they mean well." Lucy laughed. I just shook my head and got into her car. She passed through town, and I wasn't sure where she was taking me. "I know of a boutique shop that has some lovely dresses that will work."

"Oh, thank you. I just want to look nice and have a few pictures to remember the day. I don't have anyone to invite so I just wanted a small ceremony." I told her fidgeting with my purse.

"Stone and I didn't have a large wedding either. It's the marriage that matters anyway. Taker seems to be completely smitten with you and you with him so that's a good start." She pulled up outside a cute little shop with some pretty dresses in the window. We got out and went inside.

"Welcome ladies, how can I help you today?" said an older lady with a smile on her face. I started to say something when I spotted the dress from across the room. I walked straight to it and reached out to touch it. The dress was a pale pink lace over silk sheath style that would just hit me above the knees, it was off the shoulders, but the sleeves were all lace. It was absolutely stunning. I started to look at the tag when the lady snipped it off, then pulled it down for me to try on.

"Take this in the dressing room and try it on." She said pointing to the room in the back. Lucy followed me back to help.

"It probably won't fit." I mumbled as I stripped out of my work clothes. Lucy helped pull it over my head and the dress settled on me perfectly. It was beautiful. "Oh wow, I don't think I need to try any more on."

"No, I agree this is perfect. Now we just need to get you some undergarments and shoes to match." Lucy helped me out of it, and we went in search of some accessories. "That man is going to swallow his tongue when he sees you."

"Thank you for helping me and being willing to stand up for me at the ceremony. You are the only friend I have." I hugged her and stepped back. "Let's pick out a dress for you and Sarah too."

"You want Sarah to be there?" Lucy asked me surprised. "I had planned to take her to school that morning, but she could miss that day."

"We would love to have her there. Zeke adores that little girl and I want to get to know you both better." I said as I spotted a little dress in a deeper pink that would look beautiful on Lucy's daughter. I pulled it off the rack and held it up. "Is this the right size?"

"She would love that and yes, it is. Let me find a dress for myself in that color too and we will find shoes to match." Lucy looked through another rack and found a minidress in the same pink as Sarah's dress. We found shoes and some pretty tights for Sarah. After all the packages were in the car, we stopped at a men's store and found a tie for Zeke to match my dress, I picked up a second one for Axle. I trusted Zeke to take care of the rest. Lucy dropped me off at our place and helped me get the bags into the house. I hung up my dress in the nursery closet because I didn't want him to see it. Lucy walked into the nursery and smiled. She walked around looking at everything.

"We will meet you at the courthouse Friday morning, I'll help you change there, so wear something easy to get out of. I will also take care of your hair and makeup there. We can still surprise him." She winked as she left, and I smiled. I looked at the clock and saw that I had another hour before he left the shop. I went to the kitchen to find something for dinner. There were fixings in the fridge for a roast. I put seasoned it and put it in a large Dutch oven with potatoes, carrots and onions then started the stove. It should be done in a couple of hours. There was a loaf of that bread still here and it would do nicely. I stripped down and went to take a shower. After drying my hair, I braided it and then slipped on some leggings and one of Zeke's shirts. I loved wearing his clothes. I checked on the roast and then sat down on the couch with a cup of decaf coffee. I must have dozed off because I suddenly felt the cup being removed from my hand and then Zeke's lips on mine. I moaned and wrapped my arms around his neck kissing him back. He chuckled and raised up.

"Hey baby, something smells good." He said as he took a deep breath. I remembered the roast. I went to get up and he put his arm around my waist and helped.

"Dinner should be ready; I just need to pull it out of the oven." I told him but he stopped me shaking his head. He pointed to the chair and went over, grabbing some potholders and pulled the roast out of the oven. After placing it on top of the stove he turned off the oven.

"I'm going to take a quick shower, be right out." He said as he put a bottle of water in front of me. "I'll fix our plates when I get out."

I watched him walking to the bathroom, he pulled his shirt over his head, and I decided dinner could wait. I got up and followed him to the bathroom, pulling my clothes off as I went. When I got to the bathroom, he was standing in the shower with the water cascading down his ripped body. I opened the shower door and went inside with him.

"Need something baby?" he murmured as he pulled me close. I looked up at him and kissed him, fitting myself to his body.

"I need you, in me right now." I moaned as he turned me to face the shower wall and slid his fingers through my wet slit. He groaned and fit himself to me thrusting in fully. We both started moving and when he reached around and played with my clit it sent me over the edge. My legs were shaking as he pulled out of me. Zeke stepped forward and wrapped his arms around me. We washed each other and then got out of the shower to dry off.

Slipping on his shirt and some long socks I went and checked the roast, then sliced the bread. Following behind me he fixed our plates, and we sat down for dinner.

"I need to go by and pick up my suit after work tomorrow. I figured I would go around lunch time." He said as he ate. "This is good baby."

I preened under his praise. I wanted to do something for him since he was always taking care of me and I was good cook. I ate a little and then I was full. I was having to eat smaller meals now.

"I found a dress today, we also found one for Lucy and Sarah." He looked up at me in surprise. "I hope you don't mind that I asked her to be there too. I know you're very fond of her."

"I don't mind at all. She is a sweetheart, I'm sure she will be thrilled." He said smiling at me. "What color flowers would you like baby, I want to pick up a bouquet for you that morning, so I need to order them?"

"White and pink, speaking of colors I got ties for you and Axle for the ceremony." I told him nibbling on my bread. "I know it's small and at the courthouse, but I figured it would be nice to match and have some pictures."

"That sounds nice, it's our day and we will make it how we want it." He said as he squeezed my hand. "Now you relax while I put up the leftovers and clean up the kitchen. Then we can snuggle on the couch and watch a movie."

I picked something for us to watch and grabbed a blanket from the closet. Zeke brought our drinks and put them on the end table and cut the overhead light off. He reclined on the couch and then had me lay over him. I snuggled in with my face on his bare chest and that's the last thing I remember.

15

Zeke

I felt Annie's body completely relax into me, then realized she had fallen asleep. I was so content I didn't even try to move us. I just stroked my fingers through her hair and closed my eyes.

The next morning, I woke up and she wasn't on the couch with me anymore. Sitting up I listened and heard the shower. Smiling I went and changed clothes and then started the coffee. She could only have one cup, but she insisted on that one. I fixed some toast and scrambled eggs. I was putting our plates on the table when she came out of the bedroom with her stretchy jeans and a long sweater on, her long hair braided and fresh faced. Damn I was a lucky man. I held out her coffee and her face lit up. She came over and took it tilting her head up for a kiss. I gave her a quick peck.

"Eat breakfast baby, we have to get going soon." I told her. I wolfed down my egg sandwich and then went to brush my teeth and my hair. When I came back out the dishes were in the sink, and she was putting on her shoes or trying to. She looked so frustrated, I knelt down in front of her and slipped them on her feet. She gave me a smile and giggled.

"Well, I guess it's official, I can't reach my feet." She said smiling at me. "I can't believe he will be here in a couple months."

I put my hands on either side of her belly and kissed it. Laying my head on it I felt Mattie kicking. Grinning at her, I helped her off the couch. We headed to work, and I got her settled at the front desk. I had a few motorcycles to work on today. They were custom jobs so I knew I would be busy. We were taking Friday off, so I needed to get as much done in the next two days as possible. I watched Annie interact with the few customers that came into the shop. They all liked her. She was smart and very personable. I liked that she was no longer working in the bar. I hated the idea of other men staring at her ass as she served drinks. I focused on my first project and before I knew it the day was almost over. I looked over at the desk to see Annie yawning and then realized we didn't have lunch. Damnit, I finished what I was doing and went to wash up and take off the coveralls. I walked over and wrapped my arms around her.

"Baby, I'm so sorry I forgot lunch." I told her. She patted my hand and smiled.

"I ate, I had some snacks in the office. I started to try to get you to eat but Axle said you preferred not to be disturbed when you get wrapped up in a project. We need to get dinner because I know you have to be starving and I'm hungry." She slid her coat on and picked up her purse. Sliding her little hand in mine we left for the day. We drove through and picked up a pizza for dinner then went home to relax. I fixed us both something to drink and she got into some pajama pants and one of my long sleeve shirts. Rolling up the sleeves she came in and sat beside me on the couch and took a slice of pizza for herself.

Sitting back, she took a bite and moaned. I looked at her with wide eyes. She looked so happy with the pizza I had to laugh.

"Why are you laughing at me?" she asked me with her eyes narrowed. I tried to school my face and took a bite of my own. "Are you laughing at me eating?"

"Baby, you are really enjoying that pizza, I'm almost jealous." I winked at her and took another bite. "Go ahead and eat up, you might need some energy later."

We finished our pizza while half watching a show on tv. I looked over and she was curled up with an arm tucked under her head asleep. Poor baby, she was exhausted. I was going to have her take the day off tomorrow. We could catch the phone calls tomorrow. She needed to rest. I went and turned down the covers and then carried her to our bed. After slipping off her socks and pants I covered her up and went to put the leftovers in the fridge. I looked around the room after locking up and thought about how much warmer everything seemed, how much more it felt like a home again. I could hardly believe that in a few weeks we would be bringing home our son. I never thought I would have children of my own. Lisa was infertile and I loved her, so we made the club our family. When she passed, I never expected to find love again much less become a father. I turned out the lights and went to our bedroom stripping down before sliding in beside her. As soon as I laid down, she shifted over to me and threw her arm over my chest. I wrapped my arms around her and went to sleep thinking how lucky I was.

Waking up the next morning she was still curled up against me. I hated moving but I needed to get some work done today at the shop and pick up a few things for tomorrow. I climbed out of the bed trying not to disturb her. She looked so peaceful. I grabbed some clothes and went to shower and get ready for work. I left her a note on my nightstand and headed off to work.

I got to the garage as Axle was unlocking the door with a thermos of coffee in his hand. He looked up at me and nodded. I followed him in, neither of us very talkative first thing in the morning. As we flipped on the lights, I fired up the computer and checked to see if there were any invoices that needed sending out or tickets to print.

"Where's Annie?" Axle asked as he realized she had not come in with me. "Is she okay?"

"I left her to sleep; she was wiped out and I knew she wouldn't tell me. I don't want her too tired to enjoy our wedding tomorrow." I told him as I zipped up my coveralls and started working on the second bike. "I can't believe I'm getting married tomorrow."

"I know, we were all starting to think you were going to be a grizzled old hermit." Axle laughed as I threw a bolt at him. "Seriously though, we all like her. She is good for you."

"She is good for me; she gets me in a way that even Lisa didn't." I sat back for a minute reflecting on my first marriage. "Lisa was my everything for a long time. We had a lot of good times together and she was with me for the bad ones. Losing 'Sniper' the way we did really messed me up and left me with a bad taste in my mouth for running the club. I know I haven't said it, but you have done a great job as Prez since you took over."

"Thanks Taker, you know I just wanted to make you proud." Axle said as he looked me in the eye. "I'm proud to be standing up for you tomorrow, I know that Annie came into your life like a tornado, but she seems to bring calm and happiness to you. We want you to be happy."

"She will definitely keep me on my toes." My phone buzzed in my pocket, and I saw it was Annie calling.

"Good morning baby." I answered as I winked at Axle who went back to what he was doing. "Did you sleep well?"

"Why did you leave me home?" she asked me in a quiet voice. "I like working at the shop with you."

"Baby, I like having you here too. We are getting married tomorrow and I wanted you to be well rested so you can enjoy the day without swollen ankles and being too tired." I told her softly. "You were exhausted yesterday."

"I would have been okay Zeke." She grumbled. "Now I'm going to sit around this house all day bored because I have nothing to do."

"Just try to relax, binge watch one of your shows and take a nap. I'll be home before you know it." I told her smiling to myself. I knew I was grinning like a teenage boy. I didn't care, she made me feel like one again. She grumbled a bit more then hung up. I put my phone back in my pocket and got back to work on the bike.

16

Annie

I walked into the kitchen and fixed myself some breakfast. Sitting at the table I thought about my wedding tomorrow. I was getting married in less than twenty-four hours. We were going to be a family. It's crazy to think about where life takes us sometimes. I got up and walked into the room that was now a nursery. I opened the closet door and looked at my dress hanging on up. It was so pretty. The prettiest thing I have ever had, my shoes were some pretty sandals because I couldn't walk in heels right now. They were strappy and sexy with rhinestones on them. I was going to be marrying this man that had changed my life. He was gruff and grumpy sometimes, but he was also sweet, thoughtful, handsome and he was all mine. I didn't care about the age difference. I didn't have a daddy fetish or anything I just loved that he knew what he wanted and that was me. I liked that his partying days were over and that he wasn't interested in hitting clubs. I loved that he wanted to take care of me and his dominant side was super-hot. I closed the door and went to curl up on the couch and watch tv for a while.

I was nodding off when I heard a knock at the door. I sat up and looked at the clock. It was only twelve thirty. I walked over to the door and looked through the peep hole. It was Fury with a bag. I opened the door and he smiled at me.

"Mind if I come in for a second?" he asked politely. Fury was tall, tatted, bald and very imposing until he smiled, then all you saw were dimples and a handsome face. I nodded and stepped back allowing him to enter. "I had to run out and get a couple of parts and Undertaker asked me to bring you some lunch."

"Oh, that's so sweet. Thank you." I said as I took the bag he offered. "I'm starving so your timing is perfect."

"It's nothing special just some chicken tenders, fries and a small salad." He looked like he wanted to say something else but wasn't sure if he should. When I first met him, I was nervous around him. I knew he was part of the club, all the guys in the shop were. They have all been super nice since I started working there and very protective.

"Can I get you something to drink?" I asked him, then I looked up and saw him studying me. "Ok, I can tell you have something on your mind so just spit it out."

He chuckled at my attitude, I wasn't intimidated by him anymore and he knew it. I knew that Zeke would not allow anyone to hurt me, and they all cared about him so they wouldn't want to anyway.

"You're good for him. After his wife died, he lost himself for a long time. We were worried he was going to kill himself the way he was drinking, then apparently the night he met you changed everything. He may not remember being with you, but it triggered him. He got help and he has been completely sober ever since then. Since you came into his life, he has laughed more than I have seen since before Lisa got sick. She was a nice lady, a little hard from life but like a mother to a lot of the younger guys in the club. Watching her decline really took a lot out of him." Fury looked at me with a thoughtful expression on his face. "I guess I'm just trying to say, please don't hurt him. He is crazy about you, and I don't think he could stand to lose another woman he loves."

"You know, I really like you, Fury. You're a good guy. It tells me how much you think of him by coming here and telling me this. I would never hurt him. I am crazy about that man. I have not stopped thinking about him since that night. I was very hurt and embarrassed by the whole thing. I thought he just didn't want me and that I was a one and done. When everything fell apart and I needed help, he stepped up. Granted at first, he tried to throw me out on my ass but the minute he saw I was being manhandled he took over." I said biting into my fries. "We have really connected since then and are looking forward to the birth of our son."

"Well, I'm happy for you both. I need to get back to work or he's going to send a search party out for me." Fury smirked as he stood up to leave. "You need anything you let me know."

"Thank you, see you at work Monday." I told him as he went to let himself out. I pulled out my phone and called Zeke.

"Hey baby, did you get your lunch?" he asked me. "Fury is taking forever about getting back."

"He just left, he sat down and kept me company while I ate. You have great friend's honey." I took my last bite and took a drink of water. I was so full. "We have leftover pizza, why don't we have that for dinner tonight and just relax."

"Sounds good baby, I'll be home in a few hours." He said before he hung up. I smiled and put down the phone. I decided to go take a shower and shave everything in preparation for tomorrow. I wanted to be nice and clean. I could also wash my hair and then it would be easier to fix it tomorrow. I took my time with that chore and then when I got out, I dried my hair. I would get Zeke to braid it for me when he got home. I lay on the couch and fell asleep.

17

Zeke

I really enjoyed my job. Working on bikes and cars was something I had enjoyed doing my whole life and working here with some of my brothers from the club made it even better. They were good guys although many of us no one wanted to meet up with in a dark alley. I chuckled to myself. I really hoped they would find someone of their own to make them happy. I worried about Axle a lot. I planned to enjoy my life with a wife and a baby on the way it was going to be an adventure.

Lost in my own thoughts I didn't realize at first that Rider was talking to me. Until I looked up and he raised a brow at me.

"So, man, no bachelor party?" Rider teased from under the hood of a corvette he was working on.

"Nah, you know I don't drink anymore, and I have no interest in going to a strip club. I have everything I want or need at home. I'm just looking forward to making her mine legally." I said as I started cleaning up the bike I had finished working on earlier. "That baby will be here soon, and I want everything taken care of before he gets here."

"Well for what it's worth, we all like her and she has been doing great here." Rider was a good guy and didn't have a lot to say most of the time. I was glad the guys had taken a liking to my girl. She needed friends, now I just had to figure out how to get her a few more women friends. Lucy was good but she lived forty-five minutes away. I wanted her to have some closer friends.

"Maybe if you guys found you an old lady then mine would have some friends." I teased the guys. Axle had not had a serious girlfriend since Valkyrie died, he messed around and got his needs met but he had not been in a relationship. Fury had his own issues and was pretty closed off about that kind of thing. Rider was very happy go lucky but didn't seem interested in settling down anytime soon.

"Nah, don't put that kind of hex on me. I'm good with the tail I get when I need it." Axle scoffed at my suggestion. The other guys just grunted and didn't comment.

"I want to have a party to celebrate our marriage and I want the guys to attend. No whores during the party. I don't want her exposed to that. I'll invite Jesse, his wife Caroline, Stone and Lucy. I want Annie to get to know the guys because ya'll are all the family I have."

"We can do that, how about next weekend we do it, it's cold so we can't really have a cookout, but we can certainly do a chili cookoff and have several different kinds and plenty of fixings. I know that some of the guys can cook pretty well and if any of them have a girlfriend they want to bring around they can." Axle said as he rubbed his jaw. "I'll make some calls tonight, why don't you head on home, and I'll see you at the courthouse tomorrow morning."

"Sounds good to me." I said as I went and took off my coveralls and tossed them into the washing machine in the back. The guys would strip theirs off and start them. One of them would put them in the dryer in the morning. We all had two pairs each. After I washed up, I grabbed my coat and headed home to my girl.

"See you in the morning Axle." I waved as I left, climbing into my truck. It was starting to snow we were not expecting a big storm so everything should be fine for tomorrow. I wondered if Annie would want more kids or if Mattie would be all we would have. I may have to have a room added to the house. I wondered who the boy would take after. If he would have my hair and eyes or her strawberry blonde hair and blue eyes or a mix. I guess we will find out soon enough.

Pulling into the drive, I parked in front of the house. I knew that Lucy planned to pick Annie up in the morning so she could get ready at the courthouse. She wanted to have a little bit of tradition for our wedding. I had picked up my suit and it was in our closet along with the tie she had picked out for me. I could not wait to see her dressed up tomorrow. I let myself in and saw her lying on the couch. She was asleep and startled when I closed the door. Annie glanced over and smiled when she saw me. I walked over and leaned down to kiss her. She looked sexy as hell all flushed from her nap and glowing with her pregnancy. I knelt down beside the couch to talk to my son.

"Hey Mattie, have you been a good boy for Mama today?" I said as I kissed her belly. She giggled and ran her hand through my hair. I looked into her eyes and knew I was home. She was the best thing that had happened to me. My girl and our baby. I was a lucky son of a bitch. I will never forget it either.

"Do you still want leftover pizza, or should I fix something?" I asked her as I got up off the floor.

"Pizza is good." She said as she got up and walked over to me. "Will you fix me some milk please. I need to go use the restroom."

"Of course, baby, how many pieces do you want, and I'll heat it up for you." I asked her as I pulled out the box from last night. She held up two fingers before going into the bathroom. I pulled out a plate and put four slices on it and tossed it in the microwave for a couple minutes. Then poured us both a drink before setting plates on the table. She came back into the kitchen and kissed me on the cheek before sitting down to eat.

"Sorry I complained about staying home today. You were right, I needed the rest. I have slept a lot today." She blushed as she took a bite of her pizza.

"So, this is our last night before you are my wife. You still want to marry this old man?" I asked her with a wink.

"You bet I do. I want to be your wife and I want everyone to know you are my old man." She squeezed my thigh under the table and her hand crept up my leg. She was watching me as she got closer to my crotch.

"Oh no, none of that tonight. We are going to wait until our wedding night." He said as he slipped my hand into his. She pouted and started eating again. I chuckled at her disgruntled expression. My girl has had a crazy libido. "It's just one night baby, it will be better tomorrow night."

"Ok fine." She said as she sat back in her chair and rubbed her belly. She pulled my hand over and placed it on the top of her stomach. I felt movement, it was the craziest thing and such a miracle.

"Wow, that must feel so weird to you. Feeling him moving from the inside out." I looked at her in wonder. She smiled and nodded as she rubbed that spot and talked to our son.

"It feels a little weird but amazing. I can't wait until I can see him and hold him in my arms." She said with her eyes shining. "Let's watch a movie and cuddle."

"Ok honey, let me go take a quick shower and then I'll be back in a few minutes." I told her as I shucked my clothes into the bathroom hamper and climbed into the shower. I decided that I was going to shave my beard off for the wedding. I could pull my hair back in a neat style and give her a clean-shaven man for her wedding. It would sure feel weird. I would do that in the morning. After I finished the shower, I threw on a pair of sweatpants and went to the living room. She had both of us drinks on the end table and a blanket on the couch to cover up with. I picked her up and settled back on the couch with her laying against me and the blanket over us. We watched tv for a while and then I carried her to bed. It was so nice having someone to share my life with again. I didn't realize how much I missed it. All of it, the little things especially. Tomorrow will be a wonderful new start to our lives.

1
Annie

I woke up to Zeke kissing my cheek. I snuggled in for a minute and remembered, it's my wedding day. My eyes flew open, and I looked up at him and smiled.

"Good morning husband to be." I said as I kissed his lips. "I can't wait to be your wife. I need to hop in the shower soon. Lucy will be here to get me in about an hour."

"I can't wait to see you in your dress baby. You will be the most beautiful bride ever." He nuzzled my neck then got up. "Go do what you need to and then I can get ready after Lucy picks you up."

"Ok, I'm getting up." I said as I gently eased off the bed and headed into the bathroom to take a quick shower. I put my hair in a messy bun to keep from getting it wet. Once I was done, I slipped on a robe and went to the kitchen. "I need coffee and some toast."

I looked up to see him putting my cup of coffee on the table next to a glass of milk and some toast with cut up fruit. He sat down with me to eat something.

"Baby, you know I'm not about to let you leave without breakfast." He said as he ate. I polished mine off quickly.

"I need to go throw on some jeans and a button up shirt so that I can be ready to go when she gets here. No peeking." Kissing him again on the lips, I squealed and went into the bedroom. I heard the doorbell and knew it was Lucy. I heard Zeke let her and Sarah in.

"Okay baby, I will see you at the courthouse. I'm going to go take my shower so you can get the stuff out without me seeing." He said as he gave me one more hug and kiss. "Take care of my girl okay princess."

"Okay Uncle Santa." Sarah said smiling at us. "You gots to go get all handsome now."

Zeke chuckled and headed to the bathroom connected to our room. I walked into the nursery and collected my stuff.

"You ready to go get married Annie?" Lucy asked with a knowing smile. I nodded, she took one of the bags with my shoes and extras in it and I carried my dress.

We got to the courthouse and carried our stuff inside. When we walked into the bride's room there was a beautiful bouquet of daisies and roses with pink ribbon wrapped around them. A note was on the table beside them with a jeweler box. I hung my dress up and sat down to read the note first.

Annie,

This is the first day of the rest of our lives together. I can't wait to make you mine.

I hope you like the bouquet and your wedding gift.

Love,

Zeke

I tucked the note into my purse and opened the box. Inside was a pair of diamond earrings. They were so beautiful. I reached up and pulled out the pearls and slipped them in my ears. I put the pearls in the box and put them in my purse.

"No crying, we can't have your eyes all puffy. Turn around and we will get your makeup and hair done." Lucy said. She had Sarah dressed and sitting at a little table coloring. She started with my hair. She twisted it into a loose braid with curls hanging around my face. I didn't have a veil, but she produced a sprig of baby's breath to pin in my hair. It was so pretty. Then she did my makeup. It was a little heavier than I would normally wear but she said it would look pretty in the pictures. They had a photographer that was going to take some photos for us. Last, we had about 20 minutes left so I slipped on my lingerie and my garter then Lucy helped me into my dress. Last we slipped on my sandals, and I was ready.

"Okay Sarah come here; I want to get a picture of the three of us." Lucy said as she stretched her arm and took a picture of us, then took some of me alone. We snapped a few more and then there was a knock on the door. Lucy opened it and Fury was standing there in a suit. My jaw about hit the floor.

"Wow, you sure do clean up good." I said as I looked at him standing there. Lucy smiled and shook her head.

"May I have the honor of escorting you to the chapel?" he asked as he offered me his arm. I looked over my shoulder at Lucy and she giggled.

"Yes, thank you." I said as I took the offered arm and we headed to the chapel where the judge would marry us. Lucy and Sarah walked with us.

We got to the door and Fury had me stand to the side. He opened the door and escorted Lucy inside to some music followed by Sarah. The wedding march came on and I stepped in front of the doorway and almost tripped when I saw Zeke standing at the altar cleanshaven with his hair slicked back and his suit and tie on. Oh my God, the man sure cleaned up good. I walked towards him with the bouquet in my hands, never taking my eyes off of him. When I got to the front, he took my hand, and we stood before the judge saying our vows. Off to the side I saw a flash of a camera a few times, but my eyes were glued on Zeke. He slipped a beautiful diamond band on my hand and handed me his ring to slip on his finger. The judge pronounced us husband and wife and then he kissed me. Axel, Fury, Stone, Lucy and Sarah hooped and hollered at us. I blushed and laughed. I was so happy. I kept touching his handsome face completely surprised that he had shaved off his beard. I liked both but wow the difference was breathtaking.

"May I present Mr. and Mrs. Zeke Richards." The judge said smiling, he had us sign the marriage certificate and then took care of it while we went to leave. We took some pictures on the front steps and then Zeke whisked me away to a secret mini honeymoon.

19

Zeke

Seeing Annie walk to me in that slip of a lacy pink dress like a vision was something I was never going to forget. She has always looked beautiful to me but today she was stunning. I loved the look on her face when she saw me without my beard. I thought I was going to have to catch her when she stumbled but she caught herself and thankfully was not wearing heels. Now we were off to a secluded cabin for the weekend. I made sure it had a satellite phone in case we needed it.

I had her hand in mine on my thigh as I drove us to our destination. She was smiling but quiet. I think she was feeling a bit overwhelmed, and I couldn't blame her. We had a wild fast courtship due to the nature of the beginning of our relationship and we have been getting to know each other over the last month. Every day I learn things to love about her. She is kind, generous, sweet, tenderhearted and nurturing. I want to spoil her rotten. We stop halfway so she can have a restroom break. I pick up a few snacks and drinks for us while I wait for her.

When she comes out of the bathroom, she walks over to the pastry section and stares at the cinnamon rolls.

"Baby, tell them to package up half a dozen and bring them over here for me to pay for." I chuckled as the cashier boxed them up for her. We checked out and got back on the road.

"You doing okay over there, baby?" I saw her nodding off. "Why don't you scoot over here and put your head on my shoulder. She quickly unbuckles, slides over and redoes her seatbelt then lays her head on my shoulder. She yawns and I feel her slump against me. Poor baby, she is used to having a nap.

About an hour later we arrive at our cabin. It has a light dusting of snow and is very picturesque. I gently wake her so I can go open the door.

"Wait here for a minute." I tell her as I go unlock and open the door. I start a fire in the fireplace and then go collect my bride from the truck. "Ok, put your arms around my neck. I'm going to carry you."

She did as I said, and I scooped her out of the truck and carried her over the threshold. She giggled as I spun her a little before sitting her down on the couch by the fireplace.

"Be right back, I'm just going to get our bags." I told her, wrapping her in a blanket. I went out to the truck, collected our suitcase and the groceries from the convenience store and then locked it up. I came back inside to see my bride standing in front of the fireplace in nothing but a lacy peek-a-boo bra and a lacy thong. She had removed the baby's breath and took her hair down to cascade down her back and glow in the firelight. I just stood there staring at her. Then I put down the suitcase and stalked over to her. I slid my hands in her hair and pulled her in for a kiss. She tasted so good, and I wanted to taste every inch of her body. I eased her down on the rug in front of the fireplace. Kissing her sweet lips, her neck down her chest sucking her breast into my mouth. First one then the other sucking and licking her then working my way over her distended belly swollen with my child. When I reached her mound, I saw she too had a surprise. She had shaved herself completely. I breathed in her scent before swiping my tongue through her soaked folds. She tasted so sweet. I lapped at her sucking, licking and nipping until I had her writhing on the floor. She was running her fingers through my hair and clutching me to her. I looked up licking my lips and then turned her over on her hands and knees. I grabbed a pillow from the couch for her to rest against as I thrust into her hands digging in her hips as I worked my cock all the way inside her. She felt so good tightening and clenching around me as she came hard. I slid a hand around her holding her up as I thrust a few more times and released in her. She sighed and laid on the rug as I curled around her sweet body. Running my hand over her belly feeling our child there. I heard a growl come from her stomach and she giggled.

"I guess I need to feed you baby." I said as I sat up and helped her onto the couch. Walking into the kitchen I opened the fridge and found fixings for grilled cheese. I grabbed a skillet and made us a few then brought them to her. We sat and ate just enjoying each other's company. After we finished eating, I cleaned up and we went to bed. I knew she was tired.

I laid down and pulled her close to me. Kissing her on the head and she curled up with her head on my chest.

"I love you husband." She murmured to me. "I love you too wife." I replied as she drifted off to sleep in my arms. Wife, this sweet woman was all mine. That was my last thought as I fell asleep beside her.

The next morning, I woke up with my little wife kissing her way down my chest, licking my tattoos and heading straight for my morning wood. I grabbed a handful of her lush hair and watched as she took me into her mouth. I moaned as she licked the head and then twirled her tongue around me before taking me deep into her throat. Damn my wife had no gag reflex. Wasn't that nice. She looked up at me as she sucked on the head and then dove back down until her nose touched my body. She stayed there for a second before coming up for air. I pulled her off and up my body until she was sitting astride me. She sank down onto my cock and put her hands on my chest for balance. I knew it was harder for her to maneuver with her belly in the way, so I helped her by guiding her hips. I helped her ride me until she found her pleasure and screamed my name. I flipped her over and took her from behind until I finished. We went and got into the shower to get cleaned up. I was going to cook her a big breakfast to keep her energy up. I wanted to take her as much as I could because I knew that soon she may not feel up to it and when she had the baby it would be at least six weeks before we could do anything. I was always hungry for her.

I was in the kitchen cooking breakfast when she came out of the bedroom in her leggings and hoodie. She had slipped on her boots and was walking to the door.

"I just want to step out on the porch and look at the snow. I won't stay out long." She said as she closed the door behind her. It really was beautiful. Maybe we could watch the snow from the porch later wrapped up in a blanket with some hot chocolate. I had just pulled the biscuits out of the oven when I heard her scream. Then nothing. I turned the oven off and rushed to the door in time to see her being dragged off in the woods. I recognized the bastard from the night she came to the compound. I grabbed my boots and coat and took off after them.

20

*A*nnie

I was standing on the porch looking at the scenery. It was just snow-covered woods, but it was so peaceful out here. I forgot to grab a blanket when I came out and I was starting to get cold, so I turned to go back in the cabin when I felt a hand go around my mouth and an arm around my waist. I bit down, he released my mouth and I screamed then he hit me over the head. I felt like I was going to black out. I didn't see his face, so I had no idea who had me or why. My head felt all swimmy, but I didn't want to pass out. I needed to stay strong for my baby. He was mumbling under his breath and cussing. I heard Zeke take off out the door and I knew he would come for us. The asshole dragging me started moving faster and I couldn't keep my feet moving that fast. I decided the best thing I could do was to let my weight go and hope he lost his hold on me.

I let myself go limp and he lost his hold of me. As soon as he released me, I ran. I didn't know where to go I just needed to get away from him before he hurt us. It was hard to run with my stomach so big and I already felt off balance. I just had to keep moving.

"You stupid bitch, all I wanted was a little tail and instead you got me kicked out of the club and fired. I'm going to take what I want then I'll pass you around to my friends. When they are done, I'm going to cut your brat out and dump it on the Undertakers doorstep." He ranted. I realized it was the biker from the night I told Zeke I was pregnant. The man that tried to rape me. I didn't even know his name. I was getting tired, and I was looking for a place to hide when he caught up to me. He tackled me to the ground and started to drag me by my hair. I was screaming and crying when Zeke came into sight looking like a madman with a gun in his hand. I saw him and suddenly I was no longer being dragged. The asshole dropped my hair as he fell to his death. Zeke made it to me a second later and made sure the man was dead. He picked me up and took me to the cabin. Stripping us both naked, he pulled me under some blankets in front of the fireplace to warm me up. As we both got warm, he reached for his phone and sent a message. Then he took me to the bedroom and tucked me in.

"Baby, stay here. I'm not going anywhere I just have to wait for a couple of the guys to get here to clean up the mess and get rid of him. Are you okay?" he asked me as he touched my face reverently.

"I'm fine now that I'm warm and Mattie is kicking so he is fine. You can take us to be checked out after they get rid of him. We can just say I went for a walk and got lost." I said as I pulled him down for a kiss. "Why don't you stay in here with me until they get here."

"Okay love, I can do that." He said as he sat on the covers but pulled me close and held me. I must have fallen asleep because I woke up to voices in the other room. I recognized Fury and Axle. The third voice sounded like Doc.

"Well, there she is. How are you feeling little mama?" Doc said as he came over and took my temperature. Then he listened for the baby's heartbeat. When we heard it, I felt the tension in my body release. "I think you both will be just fine. Get some warm liquids into her and keep her hydrated. When she is rested get her home."

"Thank you for coming all the way out here Doc." I said weakly as I laid back against the pillows. I was suddenly exhausted.

"No problem, when you get home later Undertaker will bring you by my office and we will do an ultrasound. It will make you feel better to see him on the screen." Doc patted my hand and then went to talk to Zeke. I watched them thinking that Doc needs a girlfriend. He was so handsome, thick curly hair, pretty hazel eyes. The whole five o'clock shadow thing working for him. I think I drifted in and out of sleep for a while until Zeke came back to the bedroom.

"Baby, I have packed everything up in the truck. I have a blanket and pillow in the front for you to wrap up in. I want to get you home so we can get you checked out more thoroughly." He helped me get dressed in some dry clothes and socks then he picked me up carrying me to the truck.

"Thank you for planning a mini honeymoon honey. I'm sorry that guy ruined it." I said sadly. Zeke sat me down on the seat of the truck and took my face in his hands.

"Baby, you are alive and so is Mattie. That's all that matters. We will eventually have a real honeymoon after he is bigger. All I want is for you both to be healthy. Now let's get home so I can take care of you." He said as he got in the truck, and we headed back to Liberty. I was dozing most of the way there when suddenly I felt wetness between my legs. I looked down and saw liquid and some blood on the seat and panicked.

"Zeke, we have a problem." I said and then I screamed as a sharp pain hit me like a freight train bearing down. He looked over saw the blood mixed with liquid on my thighs and the seat. His face visibly paled, and he used his hands free to call Doc.

"What's wrong Taker? I thought you were on your way home." Doc asked and then he heard me scream again. "Oh, well hell. How far are you from the closest hospital?"

"I don't know damnit, but she is in pain there is blood and a lot of fluid." Zeke growled. I knew he hated feeling helpless. I was starting to feel another contraction.

"Look guys I don't think we have that kind of time. My contractions are coming really close together. I'm going to need to get these leggings off." I said before another scream ripped from my throat.

"I see a sign for St. Joseph Hospital in Denver, we are only about 10 minutes from it. I'm going to try to make it." Zeke said as he reached over for my hand.

"Okay, I will call ahead and have them ready for you. Annie, I want you to take some deep breaths and release them slowly. Try not to push. It sounds like your contractions are about 5 minutes apart. If you can ease the leggings off that would be good, if not I'm sure they will just cut them off. Hold on to Zeke's hand or leg to squeeze. I will meet you there." Doc said as he hung up to call the hospital.

"Baby, how are you hanging in there." He said calmly looking at me with wild eyes. I knew he was scared. I was focused on my breathing and felt another one hit as I moaned and squeezed his leg. "Look up ahead. Hold on for me baby we are almost there."

He pulled in front of the emergency room doors and jumped out. He went around to get me and carried me inside.

"My wife is in labor; contractions are less than five minutes apart and there is bleeding. We need help now!" he shouted as he carried me. A couple of nurses grabbed a stretcher and helped me on it. They rolled me back to a room with Zeke hot on our heels.

"Sir you need to fill out the insurance forms." A nurse said to him. He had a murderous look on his face.

"I'm not leaving her side, if you want them filled out then bring them to me." He said firmly.

"I don't have insurance Zeke." I reminded him. I screamed as another contraction tore through me then I was feeling the need to push. "He's coming now."

The doctor walked in and looked at me. "The baby is crowning, don't push yet." He rolled a stool over to me and checked for the cord. "Ok, looks good next time you have a contraction bear down and push."

Zeke supported me from behind holding me up, I felt the pressure and pushed. I felt him slip out and then I paused to breathe. Suddenly our sons' screams filled the room. I felt the need to push again. When I did, I felt something else come out and then the nurses started to clean me up.

"Congratulations you have a son." The doctor placed him in my arms, and he was the most beautiful thing I had ever seen. I looked down at our son in my arms and tears poured down my face. I looked up at Zeke and he was crying too.

"Baby, I can't believe you gave me a son. He is so beautiful." Zeke kissed my head and then kissed Mattie's head too. He was sitting on the bed beside me. The nurses finished cleaning me up and then gave us a few minutes with our son.

"Do you have a name picked out for him?" the nurse asked us. I nodded and looked at her.

"Matthew Zeke Richards." I said as I kissed my baby's forehead. The nurse smiled and told us she had to take him to the nursery to get his weight and finish his tests. I was so tired I didn't hear Doc come into the room twenty minutes later.

21

Zeke

I was sitting on the hospital bed holding her when Doc came in. He smiled when he saw us. I knew he saw our son because they had to have passed in the hallway.

"Looks like you have a beautiful son. He has a great set of lungs on him too." Doc chuckled. He walked over and looked at her vitals. "I bet she is wiped out. With all the excitement from the last twenty-four hours."

"Will he be, okay? He was so little, and he is six weeks early. There was so much blood." I was still freaked out because they took him out of the room so quickly.

"He will be fine, he seemed to be a good size for being a month and half early. They may keep him in NICU for a while depends on how developed his lungs are." Doc said quietly. "I'll go check on him myself if it will make you feel better. I'll also let them know you have a doctor close by to keep an eye on him when he goes home."

"Thank you. Will you take my keys and move my truck before they tow it." I tossed him my keys.

"Sure will. I'll also go by the house and get your go bag." Doc offered.

"That's in the truck too, it's a blue duffle." I said as I yawned. "They are coming to move us to another room so just check in at the nurse's station. They want to keep her for a few days to make sure there are no complications."

"Okay, if you are sleeping, I'll leave it by the bed." Doc said as he ran his hand through his hair and left.

A nurse's aide came in and got her into a wheelchair taking us to a regular room. When we got there, they gave me a hospital gown and a pair of panties with large pads for her. I helped her shower and got her settled back in bed. A few minutes later they rolled a crib with a special light into the room with our boy. They explained that he was very well developed for being early. He was only four pounds and 3 ounces, but his scores were good. They wanted to establish that he is eating good and can sit in a car seat without issues. Damn, I shot a text to Doc that we would need an infant car seat. We had planned to start getting those things but had not had a chance.

They kept us for a few days and then released us to go home. Lucy called and assured me the everything was ready at the house. She said Doc had a spare key made and took it to her. They wanted to be sure everything was set up so we could rest when we got home. After getting my little family settled into the truck, I drove us home. We pulled up to our house, a welcome home sign on the front door, balloons on the railing. Annie smiled ear to ear when she saw everything. I came around and helped her out of the truck and then took our son out with his car seat. We walked in and there was a bassinet in the living room that had wheels, it was cute. Annie sat on the couch and reached for Mattie. I handed him to his mother so she could nurse him. There were gifts and cards all over the table and I walked into the nursery to see it all decked out. The changing table had everything you could imagine. There was a note on the fridge saying they would all be by to see the newest Ripper after we had a chance to rest.

Annie placed Mattie in the bassinet and got up to use the restroom. She then looked around at everything.

"You have a wonderful family Zeke. I can hardly believe all of this." She said as she wrapped her arms around me.

"They are your family too now wife." I said winking at her. She grinned at me and then we heard a light knock on the door. I went to open it and there was Stone, Lucy, Sarah and a young woman with them. Not far behind I saw Fury, Axle and Rider. I knew the others would filter in eventually.

"Congrats, I am dying to see him." Lucy said quietly as she walked over to the bassinet to look at our son. "He is so handsome. Look at all that dark hair. I hope you don't mind, I brought Claire with me. She is Sarah's tutor and is looking for work as a nanny. I told her you may need help occasionally and wanted you to meet her."

Claire smiled and shook our hands and then stood by Sarah. I noticed Fury watching her. She glanced up at him eyes widened then she blushed and looked away. Interesting, I may have to give that some encouragement. She was young, with hair so blonde it was almost white, she had pale blue eyes, curvy and exactly his type. Annie noticed and glanced at me with a wink.

"Claire, I would love to get to know you. I'm sure I could use some help with Mattie when I get ready to go back to work." Annie said with a smile.

Everyone took turns peeking at Mattie until he woke up ready to eat again. They all excused themselves and left us to bond as a family. I just hoped that soon some of my friends would find women of their own. I can't imagine my life without my wife and son. I was truly blessed.

The End.

Made in United States
Troutdale, OR
05/17/2024